T0341751

# The Day Aunt Gina
# Came to Town

A Novel

# The Day Aunt Gina
# Came to Town

## A Novel

John Schoneboom

ROUNDFIRE
BOOKS

London, UK
Washington, DC, USA

# CollectiveInk

First published by Roundfire Books, 2025
Roundfire Books is an imprint of Collective Ink Ltd.,
Unit 11, Shepperton House, 89 Shepperton Road, London, N1 3DF
office@collectiveinkbooks.com
www.collectiveinkbooks.com
www.roundfire-books.com

For distributor details and how to order please visit the 'Ordering' section on our website.

Text copyright: John Schoneboom 2024

ISBN: 978 1 80341 754 7
978 1 80341 776 9 (ebook)
Library of Congress Control Number: 2024930519

A CIP catalogue record for this book is available from the British Library.

Design: Lapiz Digital Services

UK: Printed and bound by CPI Group (UK) Ltd, Croydon, CR0 4YY
Printed in North America by CPI GPS partners

We operate a distinctive and ethical publishing philosophy in all areas of our business, from our global network of authors to production and worldwide distribution.

For Abby and Oscar and Maisie

# Chapter Zero

Questions abound. Who is or isn't Aunt Gina? Can she be found and, if so, where? When? What century? How many Aunt Ginas are there? How many true, how many false? At its most essential formulation: is she or isn't she? And for every question, a dozen theories or more.

Aunt Gina is nothing but a figment. Aunt Gina is real. Aunt Gina was real at one point but is now symptomatic of delusion. Aunt Gina was conjured for convenience but has become real, whether by coincidence or causality. Aunt Gina is a thinly veiled excuse. Aunt Gina's use or disuse as an excuse neither impugns nor corroborates her tangibility. Aunt Gina exists as certainly as love and generosity and devotion, like Santa Claus, and subject to the same caveats. Aunt Gina has certain connections that preclude a dispositive identification under that name. Aunt Gina is as real as a kick in the nuts.

An example will help clear up just how unclear it all is. Believing young Aunt Gina to be a blackmailer and the very daintiest thing under a bonnet, a drunken-looking side-whiskered fellow with an ordinary plumber's smoke rocket in his pocket follows her into a coffee shop one morning and sits to observe. Already we don't know if it's 1888, 1988, or 2088. Europe? The new world? Another world?

The rumpled man is a detective. Incognito. He refers to Aunt Gina with a certain emphasis as *the woman* – as if she represented a certain ideal. However, this is neither pure admiration nor unseemly obsession. It is begrudging in its respect, for this Aunt Gina – if indeed it really is the Aunt Gina in whom we are interested – has already outsmarted the detective once, an unwelcome eventuality he had not previously considered possible.

1

Satisfied by her freshly clipped fingernails with lingering traces of soil, the parallel scuff marks on her shoes, and her impatient glance at her pocket watch that she has been in some muck, has a less than suitable maid, and is awaiting a companion, the ill-kempt and disreputably clothed detective sidles past her disapproving side-eye and disappears into the gentlemen's toilet. He emerges not two minutes later in the baggy-trousered garb of an amiable and simple-minded nonconformist clergyman, complete with white tie. His affected look of genial benevolent curiosity belies the smug satisfaction he feels at managing another successful disguise.

He has not yet settled definitively on a theory of Aunt Gina's game. Tentatively, he posits that she may be a geophysicist by training and related to the third daughter of one of the Schlumbergers with banking interests destined to be essential to the oil industry. If so, she may also serve as hostess for the monthly lunches of a loose-knit collection of atomic energy and electrometallurgy executives. He suspects her complicity in the Atkinson brothers' affair and knows her to be holding incriminating photographs of the king of Bohemia.

Having surveyed the café and noted telling details of structure, décor, and clientele at one unerring glance, he swiftly produces and launches the smoke bomb and cries fire, keenly homed in on our Aunt Gina's initial reaction to the apparent danger. In an emergency everyone will hasten to protect whatever it is they consider most valuable. What will Aunt Gina hasten to protect?

When the smoke clears, the detective is in his normal tweed-suited attire with a pipe in his hand. Aunt Gina? Gone. In her place a note: "Nice try." The detective's admiration becomes deeper and more begrudging. The truth is he has not been in top form since the confounding results of the double-slit experiment, but that is not our concern here. The detective exits. We will see no more of him. Nothing is settled. Things are murkier than ever.

One thing and one thing only is certain: We know whose aunt our Gina is supposed to be.

# Chapter One

Dreams? Yes: Matalulu had them.

"Of course!" Bapa Jim had said to her while they were courting. "You've got the voice of an angel!"

Bapa Jim was being charming, naturally. Later on, after they'd gotten married, Matalulu made shy noises about maybe doing that singing thing they used to talk about. Just in small clubs. Bapa Jim would laugh and once again encourage her generously in such a way that she could never pursue it. She spent years listening to records and singing along when nobody was home, or sometimes if it was just the children, when they were little. Singing and maybe sashaying a little, snapping her fingers, feeling jazzy. Dreaming.

Lately, however, she had been tolerating certain quiet ideas – more than tolerating them. She'd been more than idly thinking about the cabaret. She'd been secretly more than half-planning to go down there. Check things out. See how it's done. Speak to people, make their acquaintance. Besides, there were casinos down there. She'd always liked the slots, hitting buttons and watching small amounts of money disappear as if into the pit of a stomach. She liked the atmosphere and the drinks they gave you for free.

Obviously, the plan was even more fun because it was so secret. Everyone is entitled to secrets. Everyone has them.

Bapa Jim sold advertising for newspapers and read voraciously, but he had spent the day secretly with flamboyant pot-bellied men in top hats, bloated with brandy, inserting secret clauses into treaties, clauses that went entirely contrary to the bits everyone else was allowed to read.

Saho, their son, nearly forty now, had a million tiny secrets. Everyone had eventually learned about the liver transplant waiting list but only Bapa Jim had discovered that Saho's plastic water bottles were secretly still full of vodka.

Nor was Bahena, their daughter, a youthful forty-three, an exception. She had just that week lost her job and didn't want anyone to know. Also, she used to pull the legs off of spiders well past the age when it could be easily written off as childhood madness.

It was dinner time. Sunday, when Bahena often came round to join the others. She was the only one who lived somewhere else. Saho used to. He'd been out in the grown-up world. He was back now.

"Hey!" said Bapa Jim between mouthfuls. "I've got one for you. Check it out. Check it out."

"Here we go," said Bahena, already smiling.

"OK, check it out," he continued. "The space race. Right? The space race. An American scientist meets a Russian scientist. You with me?"

"We are with you," said Matalulu.

"Hundred percent," said Saho, instinctively; he had been elsewhere; he had not registered what was going on.

"OK," continued Bapa Jim. "So the American has the latest technology, he's real proud of himself, proud of his country. Why not? Why shouldn't he be? It's top notch. The best. So he says to the Russian, hey, comrade, check it out. He holds up a pen. Know what this is, he says. Russian says, looks like a pen. Not just any pen, says the American guy, and he's just beaming by now, he can't wait to get the next words out. It's a zero-gravity pen he says. Zero-gravity pen. Writes in zero gravity. Upside down, sideways, you name it. Nice, says the Russian. Want to guess how much it cost, says the American. Looks expensive, says the Russian. You bet it's expensive. A million dollars, guesses the Russian. A million? The American laughs. For this pen? This is a zero-gravity pen, works in space, upside down. Try eighty million dollars. This is an eighty-million-dollar pen. That's NASA for you. First class all the way. You guys have anything like that? Huh, do you, huh? The Russian shrugs. You know what he says? Any guesses?"

Everyone was smiling, nobody had any guesses.

"He says: We use a pencil."

Bahena shot some milk through her nose, which was very satisfying for Bapa Jim. Matalulu laughed so Bapa Jim could hear it. Saho smiled and felt like he missed the beginning: what was going on? What was so funny about a pencil?

When dinner was done, stout Matalulu, hair retouched, glint in her eye, excused herself to go off to visit her unwell putative Aunt Gina whom nobody had ever met. Matalulu smoked a cigarette secretly in the car on the way, occasionally emitting a grotesque series of coughs without even knowing it.

Unemployed Bahena, neatly and conservatively dressed, well fed, blonde, rosy cheeked, ordered a limousine service out of substantial reserve funds to carry her across the river where she lived alone in a large house she liked to believe was haunted.

Saho, skinny arms and legs, pudgy belly, living with his parents like he did when he was a child, offered to do the dishes. He liked to make himself useful around the house, knowing that he wasn't good for much of anything outside it, knowing he'd made a dirty hash of everything.

Bapa Jim, trim and gray, light on his feet, retreated to his study to pour himself a small glass of port, examine maps, and implicitly threaten the czar on the telephone. By the time he emerged from his study hours later and found Saho in his usual unconscious heap on the floor, Bapa Jim didn't even try to move him onto the bed. He did put the cap back on the plastic water bottle so it wouldn't get knocked over and spill. Then, on second thought, he took the cap off again, went into the kitchen, and poured its contents down the sink. Yet again, yet again, yet again. He wouldn't mention it to Matalulu when she came home. What was the point? This fellow, his son, would either sort himself out or he wouldn't, and that would be that. Hopefully he would. It was in the hands of the great elsewhere.

# Chapter Two

Did she even have the repertoire? Was she aware that she'd need more than four hours' worth of material and be able to respond to requests and know what key to sing them in? Did she have any idea what it takes to survive in the cutthroat world of cabaret singing? What was she going to do, get a personal manager? And who would take her on? She was, she was keenly aware, a nobody. Would she get by on her own initiative? Did she have a rolodex full of venue managers, booking agents, and musicians? Did she know anything about developing a marketing plan? Making a budget? Cutting a demo? Getting head shots that pop? Saturating social media?

Matalulu had not gone to any Aunt Gina's. She had cruised down the coast to the land of casinos, flicking all of her doubts out of the window one by one with her cigarette butts. Obviously, she sang in the car. She didn't just sing the songs, she delivered them, just like she did in the house, just like she'd done since the children were little. She'd get out there and sell them with style, whatever else she was doing at the time. The records would be on, and there would be Matalulu with a sly half smile, tidying here, cooking there, but singing, moving her hips, with jazzy sashay finger-snapping verve, living in two universes, one of them ghostly.

*Do you know the way to San José?*
*I'm gonna be a hat check girl at Sardi's East.*
*When wilt thou save the people?*
*In other words darling kiss me.*

Her children would often bear witness to these displays. Their experience of it was much unlike Matalulu's.

"Oh yeah," Matalulu would think, finger snapping away.

"Jesus Christ," would think her children.

That was long ago.

This was now. Matalulu arrived at the land of casinos, parked her car, and followed her nose to a little joint called The Broken Goose. She'd seen it before because she'd been to this town before, for the slots. It always seemed the right sort of place, not too grand, not too run down. The kind of place where a person might be able to wrangle an evening on a stage, maybe start a career. There was a sign outside advertising Madame Dandelion, cabaret artist. Matalulu could walk right in there and get started with the meeting people, getting the old ball rolling. She paused with her hand on the handle of the front door and let a wave of panic roll through her body.

Perhaps a casino first to get in the mood. After a short, brisk stroll away from the cabaret life she entered Lucky Lucca's. The world inside Lucca's had different air pressure, and it sounded nothing like the outside world. These were sounds by which to float. The designers of this casino were professionals. They knew how to instill and sustain a flow state. It had all the elements of cacophony but one. It had the thousands of different sounds. Beeps and bleeps and bloops and chirps and splurts, plus subwoofer richness in low burps and waves, all coming from a thousand different machines at a thousand distances, different in every way but one, different lengths, different vibratos, different pitches, different volumes, patternless. One thing held it all together, and that was that every note, every sound, every beep and bloop, was in the happy happy key of C. Gentle, propulsive, load-bearing. The overall counterintuitive effect was sensually massaging, relaxing, hypnotic, rather than jarring, repulsive, demented.

Visually, too, this world was a cerebellum-hijacking hypno-web from which escape would take some doing. One giant boundless room with an amaranthine patterned carpet, multicolored without being garish, a psilocybin sea suggesting the essence of Hinduism. The machines were not uninterrupted grids, but rather were arranged into neighborhoods that let out into circular open spaces, plazas, connecting lines suggested but not drawn, seducing the brain into adding inference to the implied. No windows. No clocks. A predominance of blue light, simultaneously comforting and paralyzing, was punctuated by sexy high-speed glamor reds near the slots themselves. Seen from one of the luxury ergonomic chairs that fronted each machine, their low-glare insistence encouraged a certain pace of button pushing in the midst of all the serenity.

The designers had not neglected the olfactory dimension. The casino pumped out a certain scent, nothing that would make you wince, a product of science, a scent that reproducible tests had proved yielded fifty percent more in revenues than unscented casinos. A hint of rose, a hint of jasmine, a touch of saffron, a bit of *je ne sais quoi*. A trade secret.

Matalulu, like everyone else, didn't play to win. She played to stay in the zero-gravity stream where nothing matters but the floating. She settled into the ergonomic chair, felt the urging of the red lights, and watched ten hands of poker appear at once. Time became meaningless but eventually there was a gradual dawning awareness, a slow recognition out of a thick sticky dream of a need to stand, a need to move, a need to change. Matalulu blinked several times and stretched and yawned and slapped her hands on her thighs and rose out of her cocoon. Could it really have been six hundred dollars later? It didn't matter. It was an unparalleled experience that she had deserved. Now it was time not to think upon it a moment longer, time to float across the essence of Hinduism to rediscover the portal to the other world and take her transfixed grace into the world of the cabaret.

Now with her hand once again on the door to the cabaret, having traversed the boardwalk and breathed in the revitalizing sea airs, Matalulu conjured the stare of the shaman. There would be no turning away. There was no time and the time was now. Matalulu pushed open the door suddenly and posed for a moment in the frame, in case anyone was watching. Affecting a look of generalized contempt with a touch of amusement, she walked in, telling herself over and over that she owned the place.

The Broken Goose was an intimate venue that could accommodate perhaps a hundred people or no more than four African savanna elephants comfortably. A woman stepped to the microphone and introduced herself as Madame Dandelion, *conférencier* and occasional performer. She introduced the act that was about to appear, a man who would juggle, tell jokes, and elicit pity.

As the juggler took the stage, Matalulu got up and approached Madame Dandelion by the bar.

"What's on your mind, doll?" said Madame Dandelion.

*Doll,* thought Matalulu, trying to smile only the right amount. *How fantastic.*

"I am a singer," said Matalulu. "I sing. I'm a singer."

"Hell of a nice dress," said Madame Dandelion, nodding. "You got style."

"You got style too," said Matalulu.

"Got a name?"

"Matalulu."

"That works," said Madame Dandelion. "So, Matalulu. You want something."

"No."

"Yes."

"Yes."

"Right?" said Madame Dandelion. "So, what is it? Say it out loud."

Matalulu leaned in and whispered into Madame Dandelion's ear.

"I want to be in the cabaret."

Madame Dandelion leaned back so as to appraise her new companion critically.

"No, no," she said. "Not like that."

"Not like what?" said Matalulu.

"What do you think this is? A shyness contest?"

Matalulu didn't know what to say.

"Give it some punch, some verve," said Madame Dandelion. "Don't ask me for it. Take it from me."

"I want to be in the cabaret."

"Louder."

"I want to be in the cabaret!"

"Who wants to be in the cabaret?"

"I do!"

"Who wants to be in the cabaret?"

"Matalulu!"

"What does Matalulu want?"

"Matalulu wants to be in the cabaret."

"So, what's Matalulu going to do?"

"Matalulu is going to sing in your cabaret," said Matalulu.

"Let me introduce you to Louis."

Matalulu followed Madame Dandelion across the barroom floor and up a short flight of wooden stairs to the office that overlooked the whole establishment. Madame Dandelion went straight in without knocking.

"No, seriously, come on in," said Louis, the proprietor, without looking up from his stack of bills. "Bring anybody."

"We have to hook this girl up with a time slot," said Madame Dandelion.

"You think?" said Louis.

"Hell yeah," said Madame Dandelion. "She's got star quality. Look at her."

Louis looked up for the first time.

"Matalulu is going to sing in your cabaret," said Matalulu.

Madame Dandelion tipped her head back and raised her eyebrows at Louis as if to say "See?" Louis nodded. Kept nodding. Madame Dandelion winked at Matalulu.

"Singer, huh?" said Louis.

"Matalulu sings," said Matalulu.

Louis sighed.

"You can have Tuesdays," said Louis, turning back to his stack of bills. "What do I care?"

None of these things happened at any Aunt Gina's.

# Chapter Three

Scholars have offered up numerous theories about our putative Aunt Gina. Unfortunately, so far they've established far more about what she wasn't than what she was. The possibilities that have been definitively eliminated could fill a Roman library. Kicking a dog who tried to steal her french fries was only one of the infinite number of things that Aunt Gina didn't do and couldn't have done for any number of reasons.

Here's how it didn't happen. Whoever Aunt Gina may or may not have been, she hadn't taken the train out to the beach during the off season, even though, presuming she is real in the ordinary sense, she would know that the coast is lovely at any time of year, even when it's cold, windy, and overcast, maybe even especially lovely, evoking the sublime feeling of simultaneous joy and desolation, life and death, now and forever, which simple blue skies and unquestioning warm rays can never convey.

She therefore didn't experience that ride of less than an hour on the commuter line, because she didn't make a transaction at the ticket machine, didn't stand on a platform and feel the slowness of time with nothing to do, didn't feel together or separate from the others similarly waiting, didn't bring a book to read on the journey or an apple in her bag, didn't think about whether to bring a swimsuit to brave the cold, cold ocean and feel heroic, didn't dig around the closet for the special folding beach blanket with the Velcro flap that always had sand in and on and about it, didn't thrill to the first glimpse of the sea between buildings through the train's dirty window, didn't instantly perceive the sea air with her nose the moment the doors opened at the seaside.

When she didn't get there, she didn't first take her shoes off to feel the cool sand between her toes, didn't unfold the special blanket at a spot carefully calculated to be equidistant from all other persons, didn't survey the horizon for cargo ships, didn't admire the offshore wind turbines, didn't clock the sound of seagulls in the breeze.

She didn't recall the sounds of the beach of her youth, when people went for tans, went for displays and rituals, went for exuberance and riding waves, went to put their towels down close to each other on packed stretches of white sand, the smell of sunscreen lotion, the glistening of taut bodies, proud and relaxed, party mode, coolers with sandwiches and barbecued chicken and beer, inter-towel flirtations, AM radios like they never sounded anywhere else, having become part of the wind, part of the gulls, part of the sea. She didn't close her eyes and breathe.

She didn't open her eyes to the present moment, didn't exhale and smile with a sense of acceptance of both disappointment and the way that silence always gets the last word. She didn't eye the rotunda and determine to fetch a snack.

She didn't look at all the steel and the grills and deep fryers and the refrigerators and enjoy the sight of burgers and hot dogs and mustard and ketchup dispensers and think about sauerkraut before doing what she knew she'd do all along and that was get an order of fries.

Dogs aren't always allowed on the beach but at this time of year they are. One thing that is known about Gina is that real or not she never had a dog of her own. She didn't hate them, but she wasn't on intimate affectionate terms. She didn't know about how they tilt their little heads, or how they have a lot of joy but no sense of humor, or how seriously they took their time sniffing around just to decide whether or not to squirt on something. When a little spaniel came bounding over, intent on claiming a share of the fries, its owner far behind, a tiny stick figure against the power of the wind and waves and sky, if anyone leapt up, cradling the fries protectively against her breast, and fending off the enthusiastic beast with her foot in what the owner would soon call a kick, it wasn't Gina. When the owner, shaking with rage, said that the sight of it made him want to kick the person who did it, if anyone felt devastated, felt like crying, felt ashamed, felt sorry, felt like hugging the man, felt like loving the dog, it wasn't Gina. Gina wasn't even there.

# Chapter Four

"Just going out to grab the paper, Bapa."

Bapa Jim looked up from the protractor he had carefully positioned on the map of Europe on his desk. Thoughts moved swiftly but serenely through well-organized corridors in his mind to logical conclusions, producing a skeptical squint.

"Fine."

"You want anything?"

"No, thank you."

Bapa Jim returned his attention to the task of calculating distances, routes, logistics, incursions. Saho sauntered out of the front door acting casual. Bapa Jim registered that Saho started whistling, only to stop himself. Suspicious.

Despite having twisted insides, Saho remained almost as simple as when he was little, so much simpler than his sister, unfortunately replicating certain gender stereotypes. When Bahena was little, her friendship circle was exciting, complicated, full of drama. There were squabbles, intrigues. There were manipulative girls who'd give you the cold shoulder while being super friendly to your best pal, only to be super friendly to you the next day and give your best pal the cold shoulder, as part of a plot to pit the two of you against each other, vying for the manipulative girl's favor. There were pretend friends who made false allegations about you and a boy, hundreds of strategic planning texts, confrontations in locker rooms, counter-allegations, narrative reversals, decisions that had to be made about whether to give birthday cakes. There were multiple versions of stories that had to be tactfully navigated by Miss Woods the school psychologist, with whom half the friend group had weekly sessions and the other half did not.

Saho's friend group dynamic had been different. Here's how it went with Saho and his friends: Someone would suggest they hang out; they hung out. Hang-out time would eventually end; they'd say "later" and go home. Had anyone asked him what was going on in the lives of his friends, Saho would not have understood the question.

In subsequent years Saho had briefly been an ordinary young adult. He'd had jobs and his own place to live. He'd been squarely within the parameters, even if bits of him trembled near and occasionally over the edges. He'd nearly been married, Saho had. Twice, amazingly, a testament to the charm he had once been able to manifest for sustained periods. No children. Those days – women – that was all over now. The entire regular world was closed to him now.

Saho arrived at the corner shop. Cigarettes, although a vice, were not forbidden. They were ordinary. Compared to the rest of it, they were wholesome. Vodka was forbidden. Secret. Fun. It entailed minor yet still breathtaking feats of surreptitiousness, such as leaving the house and coming back with vodka without any humiliating pants-down episodes. Music would play in his head as he did it, suspense music from 1970s television, which was before Saho's time except that time didn't matter anymore in the omni-connected age of all things present at once.

The music played in his head as he asked for the bottle, which was kept behind the counter. Would the shopkeeper object? Did the shopkeeper know? Couldn't the shopkeeper feel how wrong it was? Did the shopkeeper have a moral compass? If so, would she feel it was her business to employ it in this capacity? Would she put her foot down, inhale sharply, and apologetically but firmly announce that she could not permit the sale? Would she further advise Saho to straighten up and fly right, to get his affairs in order, to snap out of it, to grow up? No, none of it, of course, obviously. Saho was overthinking it. That was part of the game. That was why the music played in his head.

It played as he paid. Almost there! Still time for something to go wrong! Cops?! Doctors?! Pastors?! Ex-girlfriends?! It played as he strolled back home failing to look reputable. Would a car suddenly screech to a halt? Would G-Men pop out and tell him to get on the ground? Would someone from his past appear and accost him accusingly, forcing him to reveal the contents of his plastic bag? Would a manhole slide open and a scaly fish-man tentacle grab him down into the darkness?

It played louder, the music, when he approached the house and went not to the front door, but around to the side, around to the back, but not before looking suspiciously both ways with his shiftiest eyes. It played as he placed the bottle outside his window. It played as he made his way back around the front so as to enter the house in a normal fashion. It played as he looked around guiltily once more before opening the door.

"Got you a candy bar," he said upon entering, tossing the shiny wrapped peanut, chocolate, and caramel confection onto the Balkans.

Bapa Jim looked up from his map and appraised the situation with a piqued half-interest. He was not a candy bar man and Saho was plainly up to something stupid.

"Thanks," said Bapa Jim, choosing not to say anything more out of a sense of avoiding the obvious, out of not wishing to embarrass, accuse, or affront, out of side-stepping the kind of confrontation that might threaten the serenity of the home, out of a hope that the look on his face or the feeling in his heart would be perceived, would be absorbed, would be enough.

Saho went into his room, shut the door, quietly opened the window, carefully retrieved the bottle, poured the contents into an empty water bottle, placed the vodka bottle back outside on the ledge, and drank himself unconscious. No one the wiser, he smirked to himself. Super spy.

Bapa Jim took a bite of the candy bar and drew up some lies for people with magisterial airs to tell. Peanut, chocolate, caramel, war.

*Yum*, he thought. *I'd forgotten about candy bars.*

# Chapter Five

How quickly one takes for granted one's comforts. In her enormous empty house, which she told herself might be haunted, Bahena sat and felt the emptiness and imagined that she could hear whispers and things moving. Unemployment. What if the jig was up? What if this was the beginning of the great unraveling? It would be great if there really were ghosts. Figures walking in the night. The sensation of a cold hand touching her skin. Bells ringing without being pulled. The sound of carriage wheels when no carriage was there. The occasional distinct smell of fresh tobacco attributable only to the deceased old pipe-smoker who lived here a century ago and looked after horses. That would really be something. Something special.

Bahena opened a salad she had bought at the luxury supermarket and while she ate it, she thought about starvation and loneliness and being forgotten. She decided she would not be afraid if a ghost made itself known. She would be calmly receptive and ready to communicate serenely with the next world. In that steely frame of mind, she tidied and thought about who her friends really were. Which ones would come to her aid when the chips were down, which ones would distance themselves? At precisely five o'clock she opened a bottle of white wine and had two glasses, one right after the other. On the one hand, she thought, I've gulped that first one right down like a lunatic but, on the other hand, I did wait until five and I've slowed to a decent pace on number two. Times are hard, she thought. Times are bleak. Times are haunted. Times are haunted by the always-already absent-present of lost futures. She looked out of the window at the waning moon and wondered whether birds think bats are crazy, the way they fly.

Everything had been so good for so long. Oh yeah, she thought, me, the big executive, whoop-de-do, living large, not like poor Saho. Could this be karmic payback? For what? The complacency? The spiders? *Jesus, God, then I deserve it*, thought Bahena, hoping that by saying she deserved it she'd prove she didn't deserve it. She looked around. No ghosts. Two spiders. She leapt up and slammed them with a magazine, one after the other, slammed them flat. Speaking of deserving it no they didn't, she thought. *However, I did not torture them.*

Who says things can't get even worse, tumble to the bottom, turn upside down, get hellish? I might get possessed by a ghost and end up running in front of a car in a flash in the cold in the dark like a flipped-out demoniac.

She named things about herself that weren't boring. She got caught stealing when she was little and was punished, and Saho did not get caught and was not punished. That's when she said "I hate you, Mommy" under her breath and didn't mean it. Her mother heard it and slapped her and gave her a nosebleed. She still steals things to this day. There's the spider thing. Say what you will, not boring. Haunted house. Possibly. Not boring. Not boring unless you've lived forever and seen everything infinity times and you're still bored while getting sucked into the last black hole.

Bahena's reverie was broken by the phone ringing; she answered it. It was a woman called Juniper. Word had gotten out about Bahena being available, because Bahena had been a big-shot executive and when people like that get let go there are networks that jolt into action. If there's a terrible public scandal or the person has a super jarring laugh the networks protect themselves, but otherwise they protect the person.

"Yes?" said Bahena and then there were tiny cartoon voice-over-the-phone noises: wok wok wok wok wok.

"You don't say," said Bahena. Wok wok wok wok.

"Certainly, I'm interested," said Bahena. Wok wok wok.

"So, they're real?" said Bahena. "You're saying they're real and this is a real job and that's the real salary?" Wok wok.

"Monday morning is fine," said Bahena. "I look forward to joining your team."

Bahena's period of dizzying unemployment had lasted three days.

# Chapter Six

"What do you think of it?" Bapa Jim asked the naked man at his right shoulder in the dimly lit bedroom.

"I think," said Bertie, "that it's some sort of... chair?"

"An understatement."

Bertie walked slowly around the object, tracing his royal index finger along its contours as he moved, his majestic belly mercifully obscuring his turtle-head ding-dong.

"Observe," said Bapa Jim, proceeding to demonstrate the swiveling and extending of which the machine was capable, the fold-away perches it included for multiple simultaneous occupants at strategic angles, suggesting to a fertile imagination the various positions it enabled, including a few that would otherwise be absolutely impossible.

"Are you starting to get the idea?" said Bapa Jim.

"My God," said Bertie, climbing onto the device and splaying himself out in various grotesque formations as Bapa Jim tastefully averted his gaze. "It's as if it were made just for me and my imperial girth!"

"It was," said Bapa Jim. "And there is one other thing."

"There isn't."

"It's nothing. A small token."

Bapa Jim walked over to the head of the more-than-king-sized bed, where a piece of cloth had been draped over something on the wall. Bertie clapped his hands in anticipation.

"Shall we count to three?" suggested Bapa Jim.

"Three!" said Bertie. "Three!"

"As you wish."

Bapa Jim gave the cloth a strong pull to reveal a magnificent coat of arms, Bertie's own, in garish reds and blues and golds, decorated with images of a harp and lions, the better part of a meter in height, bearing the inscription, in German, *ich dien*: I serve.

"But this means..." began and ended Bertie.

"Yes," said Bapa Jim. "This is now officially your room. Your own private room at the best brothel in Paris."

"You're a good friend to me, Jimmy," said Bertie. "A very good friend."

"It's nothing."

Bertie slid laboriously off the chair into a standing position, pressed his hands together, looked upwards as if to heaven, closed his eyes, and smooshed his face out into an august pink smile.

"The king is pleased," he said.

"Then so am I," said Bapa Jim. "We do have a few matters to discuss, if you don't mind, and, of course, you may feel free to clothe yourself although that remains as always at your own regal discretion."

"Dear God," said Bertie. "I just thought, given the site of our meeting, that..."

"A natural supposition. Think nothing of it."

"Dear God," said Bertie, waddling to the other side of the room and snatching his dressing gown from where it lay on a small side table.

Bapa Jim wanted to buy his Matalulu a gift from Paris, but nobody was meant to know he'd been, so he added it to the long list of minor pleasures he would have to deny himself. He wished he could have brought Saho along too. It would do that boy good to walk along the Seine, wander the Louvre, sip a cappuccino in a wicker chair at a sidewalk table. It would do him good to get out and go anywhere, do anything, take an interest in cities, in culture, in living. Bahena? Well, it would be nice, Bapa Jim supposed, but would she want to? Would it inspire her? Would it be up her alley? Would she, to put it frankly, get it? Ah well, ah well, ah well. Business was business. Needs must. In any case it did a fellow good to be in Paris now and again, regardless. Its elegance can make you forget that these people will suddenly tear up the streets and burn everything if properly provoked.

"I am sufficiently buttered up, incidentally," said Bertie, tying the belt of his dressing gown and assuming appropriate airs. "I'm ready to be told the actual reason for your visit."

"Very good," said Bapa Jim. "It's just that some of us have been noticing that the Combined Principalities have made astonishing industrial progress under the direction of the Kaiser."

"Oh yes," said Bertie, clapping his pink hands. "He's my nephew, you know. They are seeing the fruits of his investments in education and new technologies. He puts it all into social welfare and the arts, you know. Say what you will, he looks after his people. Happiest country on earth. A well-deserved success from which we could all stand to learn a few lessons! Isn't it wonderful?"

"No, your highness," said Bapa Jim. "It is not."

"Oh," said Bertie.

Bapa Jim explained to Bertie that the Combined Principalities were a menace owing to the demands of international competitiveness and the burden of maintaining full-spectrum dominance. All the things that happen to menaces would have to happen to the Combined Principalities. There was much work to do. It wouldn't necessarily be all fun and games, it wouldn't be without its moral qualms and ethical dilemmas, but for their own futures, for their own families, for history, for posterity, because of their far-reaching vision, they had to humble the Kaiser.

"I see," said Bertie, idly working levers on his new chair. "Well, my mother is wild about him, but I can tell you I don't share the sentiment. He's a bit of a pill to be honest. Mother is always Kaiser this, Kaiser that, you should be more statesmanly, you should be less of a pig, you're such an embarrassment to the family, you're completely disgusting, have a look at that

Kaiser, now there's a man and a half. It's no wonder he's so full of himself. And he makes such a fuss at the slightest bit of cheating at cards. I don't mean to complain but you've dragged it out of me."

"You have ample reason."

"I know!" said Bertie. "But what can I do?"

"It would be ever so helpful," said Bapa Jim, "if you could find the time to attend some lavish parties and balls, travel extravagantly, gamble majestically, drink prodigiously, ride horses, visit as many country houses and brothels as you can, bestow a few knighthoods throughout Europe. Be yourself. Be likable. Be larger than life. Make friends. Let them know where you stand. Get people on board. We're going to need them. This will be a team effort. We need everyone we can get to apply the right sort of pressure. Since you happen to be here, you might even start with the French president. He'll be a key ally."

"A charm offensive."

"Exactly."

"Hurrah!"

# Chapter Seven

Everyone had gotten together for dinner, and Saho had volunteered to cook. It was one of the things he sometimes did to prove he deserved to live, to dare anyone to say he was not a respectable person. He'd made a pot roast with plenty of carrots and potatoes. Everyone's mouth was watering. Despite this accomplishment, Saho looked wobbly. Everyone convinced themselves they hadn't noticed so that nothing needed to be said. Did the smell of cheap spirits from the chef vie with the aroma from the food? Was there something unwholesome, even nauseating, about it? The dinner-ruining thought was instantly nullified, disallowed, had never happened.

Matalulu entered the dining area seeming taller and thinner than usual, paler than usual, wider mouthed, and she suddenly had flaming red hair. She was dressed not in her usual baggy blue jeans and a sweatshirt, but in a high-necked, low-hemmed clinging black dress. Everyone bounced fleeting glances off of her and decided it was best not to comment. Whatever it was might be terrifying, might implicate the need for action, might involve doctors. Matalulu sat down in her chair as if onto a throne. On the one hand she had not been praised; on the other she had not been mocked. Noncommittal silence was within the comfort zone, although it exacted a silent price. People, she knew, could get used to this. People could get used to anything.

They said grace without belief out of habit and tucked in. The recent rain was commented upon unfavorably, as was the state of the local baseball team's relief pitching. The new streaming series was very exciting and everyone was looking forward to it. There was a dictator somewhere and the table unanimously frowned upon him. The next-door neighbors were evidently having a built-in swimming pool installed; it was going to take up most of the backyard. So much for greenery.

And had anyone seen next-door's recycling bin? All the liquor bottles in it? That's a lot of drinking. Saho tsk-tsked along with everyone else.

"Hey," said Bapa Jim, smiling in anticipation of the joke he was about to tell. "Drill sergeant says to Private Jenkins, hey, Jenkins, I didn't see you at camouflage drill today. Jenkins says, Thank you, sir!"

Bapa Jim looked around expectantly, eyes wide with mirth. Matalulu and Bahena laughed.

"Nice one," said Bahena as Matalulu smiled and shook her head. Saho misinterpreted the story by way of not really listening. He thought it was a true story about a fellow called Jenkins, must've been some kind of acquaintance of Bapa Jim, unless Bapa Jim was more of an acquaintance of the sergeant, that was possible, didn't really matter, but this Jenkins if he understood correctly had skipped out on some sort of drill and was proud of it. Sounds like he was risking whatever happens to soldiers for impertinence but as far as Saho was concerned, well, he could appreciate the sense of defiance. Good luck to Jenkins as far as Saho was concerned. To hell with these military authoritarians anyway.

"So!" said Bapa Jim, having elicited desired responses from wife and daughter, having noticed the blankness from his son, wanting to say something to him, something inquisitive yet not intrusive. "Saho, my handsome son, what have you been up to today? Anything good?"

"Oh, you know, this and that. I cooked dinner."

That didn't sound like enough, even though Bapa Jim had said "mm hm" in a way that was clearly meant to sound supportive.

"I mean," he continued, "you know, I read a little, did some writing" – and here he almost said he had looked through the help-wanted ads but felt that would be gilding the lily – "working on a few things, you know."

Saho hurled a profanity at his own father for the insulting nature of the question, but only silently, inside his own head. Outwardly he kept his nose pointed at his plate and thought about whether he could answer more effectively, about what else he could say in his own defense. He decided not to mention the hours he had spent watching videos of grown men slapping each other hard in the face as part of some kind of manliness contest, or the videos of people making incredible pool shots involving unlikely banks, or the videos of the hilarious excerpts from popular quiz shows. Nobody asked what he had been reading. Nobody asked what he had been writing. Nobody asked what he'd been working on. Nobody said anything about the smell or the slurring.

"Will he be in trouble, then?" asked Saho, just to change the subject.

"Who?" said Bapa Jim.

"Perkins," said Saho. "Jenkins. The guy."

"Who?"

"The guy who didn't show up."

"Show up where?"

"I don't know."

Moving on then. Subject dropped. Bapa Jim shrugged his shoulders. He glanced at Bahena and thought about asking her what she'd been up to, but he decided that such questions were useless and besides, he was no longer in the mood to ask them. She'd lost a job, that was just going to be a bad conversation. Had she gotten a new one? Had someone said something like that? In fact, Bahena had told Matalulu and Matalulu had told Bapa Jim, but he hadn't really been listening. His subconscious whispered to him that he was supposed to know something about a job. But what? Asking was clearly impossible. It would reveal his ignorance. He'd just pick it up from clues.

Bahena didn't like to make a fuss over herself, and not only that, she resented that nobody had shown any interest in what she was up to or what jobs she might have lost or gained and the last thing she was going to do was provide a lot of personal information to a bunch of people who obviously had more important things to worry about. Let them ask if they want to know.

Saho wasn't clear about any of it but understood that Bahena and job were two words that went together and that she was in a superior and infinitely more secure economic position than he.

Matalulu surveyed the family.

"I love this family," she said with the air of a grand tragedienne, to horrified silence. "I love all of you so much."

After the mortified pause, she added: "I know I shouldn't say so. I know I'm perfectly awful. I'm a terrible person. I'm guess I'm just a crazy old lady. I should know better."

The subject was quickly changed. Bapa Jim observed for the second time how rainy it had been lately, this time adding with a wise old nod of his head that it meant the grass would be loving it. He'd have to get the lawnmower out this weekend. Stuff is growing like mad. Sure looked lush though. Bahena offered that she loved the smell of fresh cut grass; Bapa Jim readily agreed. Saho had fallen into a faraway state of unfocused glaze, but his half-open lower jaw trembled as if stupidly.

Bapa Jim had his own quiet smile, thinking about all the events he had set in motion, all the pleasing tricks and the subtlety and the cleverness. He caught himself and put his face in order. Don't be too pleased, it was no laughing matter, just better than the alternative, that's the thing. Tough man, tough job. Nothing to smile about. Don't invite inquisitiveness. Questions were known to be unlikely here but should one occur, he was ready. Even those who would not ask the questions knew what the answer would be.

"All quiet here!"

# Chapter Eight

"Your melon balls are divine," said the world-renowned singing idol Johnny Mathis from the comfort of his poolside garden chair. His tone of voice was as legendarily smooth and mellifluous as always. It had a calming, almost hypnotic, effect. Everything he said, no matter how trivial, was like a song written by liquid caramel numina. He placed his glass down gently on the white wooden folding table, peered over the top of his sunglasses, and smiled.

Matalulu, despite herself, despite her contentment and her love of family, felt her heart flutter.

"Oh, Johnny," she heard herself say. It wasn't what she'd wanted to say. There were no words that would have even been adequate. What she would have liked would be for her mouth to open and for warm colors and the sound of millions of ping pong balls bouncing quietly off Pluto to come out in a stream that felt like the harmony of all things. "I mean, yes. I mean, thank you. They're really very simple to make."

How had she gotten here? How was Johnny Mathis still only in his early thirties? How could it be that she was totally famous and still completely unknown? These were not questions that Matalulu asked.

"I want to thank you for inviting me to your concert," said Johnny Mathis. "I enjoyed our duet. You have the voice of an angel, and what a pleasure to be on stage once again at Madison Square Garden, if only for the one song. I am in your debt."

Johnny Mathis pushed his sunglasses back into place and sat back in his poolside garden chair, smiling handsomely. Matalulu, despite herself, admired his smooth chest, his dark glowing skin.

"Oh, Johnny," she heard herself say.

Then they were at dinner, at a restaurant – Italian? – sounds of glasses clinking, silverware scraping, murmuring background voices, everything out of focus except each other.

"I'm glad you asked," said Johnny Mathis. "It's all because of my father. He pushed me into pursuing a singing career. He really encouraged me. He believed in me. He supported me. Emotionally. Really, he was my best friend."

"Did you..."

"I did. I had the happiest childhood in the world. I had six brothers and sisters and we got along splendidly. We looked after each other, you know. We cared for each other and loved each other and were never cross with each other. Each of us kind and gentle to all of the others. We adored our parents. We felt their love, their support, at all times, and still do to this day. It sustains us."

"And was..."

"Not at first. Not for a long time. Because my mother was black and my father white, we had our own perspective and racism simply did not occur to us as something that might exist. Why would it? It never entered our minds. Never entered mine until I started singing and traveling through the South. I discovered that they would let me sing, but would not let me *in*. Would not let me eat in their restaurants or stay in their hotels or sit with them. There were many things I could not do at that time, in certain places."

"And did..."

"It never made me angry. It was, of course, outrageous. Nevertheless, I maintained my personal serenity. Otherwise, I could not sing. Otherwise, I certainly could not sing in the particular special way that I sing. My hypnotic and euphonious effect, it comes from within, from my well of pure serenity. I must nurture it, protect it. Inside, I must stay still, like the surface of a lake on a windless evening at sunset in a dream. To get angry would be to give them what they could not take."

"Oh, Johnny."

Matalulu reached across the white linen tablecloth, took his hand, and despite herself could not help but gaze into his deep brown eyes.

"And who's this?" said Johnny Mathis, pointing with his nose to an elderly woman who came in looking like she must be eight feet tall, which would be almost impossible. An eight-foot woman would make you question the ground on which you stood. She had on a wide-brimmed hat, a red one-piece, and a floral-patterned thin cloth wrap-around. When she smiled, she had amazing teeth.

Matalulu looked up to see who the newcomer was. She leaned in close to the smooth bronze ear of Johnny Mathis.

"Oh," she whispered. "That's just my Aunt Gina."

"*Enchantée*," said Aunt Gina, holding out her bony hand for Johnny Mathis to kiss.

Johnny Mathis kissed her bony hand. Aunt Gina smiled with her teeth.

"That's my Aunt Gina," said Matalulu out loud.

"I been sick," said Aunt Gina.

"I'm gay, of course," said the idol Johnny Mathis. "I can say it now. In those days it was quite another matter. Quite another matter indeed. But these days it's no big deal. These days everyone is gay and nobody bats an eye."

He laughed and his deep brown eyes twinkled as if they comprised the stuff of quasars. Aunt Gina was gone now, like a restless spirit finally surrendered to peace or looking for trouble elsewhere.

"Is there..."

"Not in the way you mean. I always felt that my parents had the perfect marriage. How could I – how could anyone – compete with that? So, no. I have not had a sole special someone. But I am fortunate to have many special someones, without having the responsibility of living with them."

"Aren't…"

"Not at all. Apart from my homosexuality, I am blessed to have many friends that I call buddies. We play golf. They are golf buddies. I have played with Trevino, Palmer, Nicklaus. I have a two or three handicap, which, if I may say, is not bad for someone my age."

Matalulu didn't know where she had been looking, but it was no longer into the deep brown eyes of Johnny Mathis, because now she had to turn to look back at him. He was no longer in his early thirties. He was an old man of eighty-six. A spry old man who looked very good for eighty-six.

"My son was a good boy," said Johnny Mathis.

"But…"

"He did not deteriorate into a waste of space and my daughter was lively and interesting. My husband was communicative and real. I fulfilled my ambitions. A dreamer? Perhaps. Is a man a dreamer if his dreams come true?"

When Matalulu woke up she felt very disoriented for a good few minutes. Was she in her bedroom? She was in her bedroom. Was it morning? It was morning. Was Bapa Jim in bed beside her? He was. Still asleep, until she looked at him. He opened his eyes as if he could feel her eyes pointed in his direction.

"Morning!" he said cheerily. "Hey! I've got one for you, check it, listen to this: Three statisticians go hunting. They see a deer. The first one shoots, misses five feet to the left. The second one misses five feet to the right. The third one says 'We got him! We got him!'"

Matalulu smiled. What day was it? It was Tuesday. Tuesdays were hers. Louis had said so. It had really happened. Tonight, Matalulu would be a cabaret star. Under the covers Matalulu twinkled her toes in silent excitement.

# Chapter Nine

There is no hard evidence that the girl in the polka dot dress was Aunt Gina. She almost certainly couldn't have been. She may or may not have even been in the hotel, but Aunt Gina definitely never spoke to the young man who climbed down from the rack of trays at the east end of the ice machine on the south side of the pantry; she could not have seen him head north toward the steam table.

Most accounts have the girl in the polka dot dress very happy – a little bit *too* happy – and fleeing the room with a tall, thin, dark-haired young man in a golden sweater into the adjoining main kitchen. There are, however, zero reports of Aunt Gina having been familiar with any thin, tall, dark-haired, golden-sweater-wearing men at this point in time. She knew thin men who were tall but had light hair; she knew short, fat, dark-haired men; she knew men who were light-haired and short who clearly don't enter into the equation at all. The only man she knew who might fit the description was borderline thin and had dark hair, but his height would most likely be described as medium or average rather than tall, his sweaters were reliably blue or gray, and witnesses place him nowhere near the pantry.

The problem with those who like to point to examples of a putative Aunt Gina fleeing from a nominal situation is that they tend not to mention the motivation that would be the *sine qua non* of the premise. In short, yes, an Aunt Gina had been known to flee – when *unhappy*. It's also true that there were things going on in that pantry that could have made an Aunt Gina dreadfully unhappy, with reports of injuries and projectiles and most unsettling chaos. However, as noted, the wearer of the polka dot dress, whoever she may have been, was by all accounts tending toward the deliriously untroubled.

There are a good half-dozen reports of a girl in a polka dot dress in that state of feverish cheer, running with this tall, thin, dark-haired fellow in his vulgar golden sweater – we shall refrain from calling him a flashy ne'er-do-well as we must acknowledge having insufficient information upon which to base such a damning conclusion – and bursting out of the southwest kitchen exit past a man in a maroon coat and onto the fire escape stairs.

Now, let us pause here to ask why so many people noticed this girl and her polka dot dress, and why everyone called her a girl when she was clearly not a child but a grown, albeit young, woman. Let us dispense with this second question first by noting that it was a function of the times, which is not to excuse sexism but merely to observe that, at the time in question, awareness of the infantilizing effect of using the childish term to describe an adult had still not been raised to modern standards. We need neither be apologists for history nor carry this regrettable habit into the present day and will henceforth refer to the probable non-Gina in question as the young *woman* in a polka dot dress.

Perhaps ironically, according to numerous witness reports it was specifically the woman's womanly curves that had attracted so much attention to this so-called "girl" in the first place. Did Gina have a similar attention-grabbing shape in her youth? Unfortunately, the photographic evidence is scant. We have a few grainy black-and-white images of a woman on windswept beaches and very little agreement on whether they constitute a representation of Aunt Gina at all, let alone an accurate one. In one image she does indeed appear to be sporting an ample bosom, to put it frankly, but at least one cetologist has attributed the effect to what may be a partially obscured background dolphin in mid breach. In support of this theory, a second photograph can be produced, evidently taken either moments before or moments after the first, in which an offshore pod is arguably visible and the angle on the woman inconclusive. The paucity of photographic material has been cited by some of the more paranoid historians as suspicious in and of itself, as if to suggest that nefarious record-wipers have been at play. The accusation holds little water, however, especially when we consider that the ubiquitous mobile devices of today were nowhere near as prevalent during Aunt Gina's presumptive bloom. Regrettable, but hardly probative.

The other notable feature of the young woman in the polka dot dress mentioned by practically every witness was her nose. Variously described as "upturned," "pug," "funny," "broken at some point," "might have been fixed," "like a pixy," "short," "large," "long and thin," "crooked," and "thin between the eyes, broadening below, narrowing again at the base, only to widen at the nostrils somewhat." Everyone agreed it was memorable. Most thought she was "cute," "attractive," or "very attractive" with her adorably unconventional nose and her "good figure," but one holdout maintained that she was "not that pretty, actually" while conceding the point about her figure. This was a time, it must be recalled, when the use of the term "figure" to refer to the broad physical outlines of a woman was considered normal. It may sound dated to our more sophisticated ears but at the time it was shapely girls with good figures all the way.

In any case, our only recourse to Aunt Gina's ostensible nose is by inference, thanks to the aforementioned scarcity of reliable images. An acknowledgement of a certain Uncle Arthur may be merited with reference to this issue, if only in passing. A gentleman of a certain avuncularity named Arthur who wore wool suits and a herringbone newsboy cap claimed to have been familiar with Aunt Gina for a time while they were both in high school, or in their early thirties, or in a previous existence as early hominids or disassociated elementary particles, depending on when he was telling the stories and frankly how many pints he'd had. An obviously outlandish and unreliable witness, Uncle Arthur and his testimony are notable only because the one feature of alleged Aunt Gina about which he waxed eloquent was her nose. That he held it to be ramrod straight and unnervingly perfect with a sharpness that could be used, if only the requisite angle were obtained, to slice cheese is, of course, not in itself any guarantee that she never wore a polka dot dress in a hotel pantry. The burden of proof remains on those who would insist it was so. Her extant suppositious blood relatives' noses, not least of which were those belonging to Matalulu, Bahena, and Saho, were of such variety as to be virtually useless in establishing a likelihood one way or the other. "Noses may run," as one wag from the Rosemont Institute put it, "but not in families." We shall leave the arguments to the geneticists.

In any case, on the fire escape this voluptuous young woman in a polka dot dress is said to have shouted things, made unsolicited commentary, as she passed the man in the maroon coat, an act that is as un-Gina-like as any we can imagine. The Aunt Gina of legend is a demure figure who would be about as likely to shout at a maroon-coated man as she would be to attack a gorilla with an electric bass.

Nor were the polka dots – uniformly described as black or dark violet circles about the size of a quarter against a white background – remotely similar to anything in Aunt Gina's wardrobe as catalogued in *The Clothes of Aunt Gina*, a notebook reportedly compiled by Matalulu's mother, Angela. While it is true that Angela denies any knowledge of said notebook, both the book and verified examples of Angela's shopping lists were written in handwriting, suggesting, at a minimum, a similarity in technique. Angela's denials must always be taken with a grain of salt in any case; she once denied eating the last of the good apples even though a fresh core, still glistening, was sitting on the spotty table next to the very chair upon which she was sitting at the time. For what it's worth, the notebook documents an orange scarf with white polka dots as well as a green dress with yellow lemons of various sizes. Some authors have tried to conflate either or both of these sartorial wonders with the white dress with quarter-sized dark polka dots, but the amount of clear, consistent, contrary testimony that we would have to consider erroneous would strain the credulity of any reasonable person.

The evidence that Aunt Gina and the young woman in the polka dot dress are one and the same person begins to look very thin indeed. The best we can say for this beleaguered theory is that the woman in the polka dot dress may have been an aunt, and she may have been a Gina, but the odds of her being Aunt Gina are worse than you'd get for a left-footed lemur getting hit by a bus driven by a lottery winner on a baseball diamond in December. It is past time to drop this discredited line of inquiry entirely.

# Chapter Ten

Saho crept into the kitchen looking for a snack. Why creep? Why not walk boldly forth? Indeed, why not sashay? Because Saho was not proud of his trip to the kitchen. The whole way there from his room he felt worse and worse and had to keep attacking the idea of turning around, of not going into the kitchen, he had to punch and kick that idea until it was all smashed and made him sick. He felt it as sure as he felt the ground under his feet, felt self-loathing, a self-loathing that poked him over and over again whenever he did something that he loathed about himself, poked him without pause, right in the forehead, mercilessly, like an insane child-devil from the sort of movie he couldn't even watch anymore.

For one thing, he knew he'd been putting on weight. There was no denying that at this point. His food-to-exercise ratio would not bear scrutiny. His exercise regimen was such that he would sometimes look up on computers the number of calories burned each day just by one's heart beating normally. In this he found solace, for although he could never find a precise reliable figure, the number was certainly greater than zero. Typing – looking things up – that didn't happen without some amount of energy. There was a bit of walking involved in his day. He'd go from his room to the living room or the kitchen, and occasionally – perhaps two times every three days – all the way to the local shop, a good quarter mile away. That would all amount to something, although not, perhaps, to a single pork chop.

He was a tall man, over six foot by a generous margin. As a child he was thin as a rail. Now, however, he looked fat. *Un poco gordo.* He *felt* fat. Not enormously so. His arms and legs were still skinny, even too skinny. But his belly was not the taut flat plain of his teenage years. There had been a long period of sucking it in, loosening trousers, buying bigger sizes, convincing himself that it was the sizing system that had changed, but that was all over now. No more sucking it in. He had relaxed into his belly. He had given it up, transcended vanity, embraced shame. He was letting it hang. He felt sheepish, going into the kitchen, looking for snacks, but on the other hand, he was hungry. Was he hungry? What was this hunger, a need or a desire? In any case, Saho the philosopher wanted a snack.

He opened the cupboard and took out some chocolates and some crackers. He opened the fridge and took out some cheese and some sliced turkey. He opened the bread box, took out some crumpets, put them in the toaster on its highest setting. Then he felt a little bit thirsty all of a sudden and he opened the fridge again.

He knew what he was going to do and it was something he wasn't supposed to do. He picked up the orange juice and kept the fridge door open. He paused to listen attentively. Was anyone coming? Was there any chance he'd be caught red-handed and suffer embarrassment?

No. There'd be doors and steps and floorboards and all sorts. No creaks. Nothing. He shook the bottle vigorously and listened again. Still nothing. He was alone. Nobody was coming. He was good to go. It was just him, his conscience, and some juice.

Instead of pouring some into a glass, Saho put the orange juice bottle directly to his lips and gulped and gulped and gulped some more. Looking left and right shiftily just to make double sure he'd not been seen, he replaced the orange juice and shut the fridge door. Mission accomplished. *Ha.*

Ahhh, he said. And then he took his snacks, snuck back into his room, watched hockey on his little television set, and drank vodka from a water bottle until he passed out.

If anyone found him, they'd think he'd been drinking water. That's what people think when they find somebody passed out next to a bottle with a water label on it. It fools them every time. They might initially have contemptible suspicions and accusatory notions about the person having drunk themselves into another stupor, but when they saw the name-brand water bottle they'd go no, I guess not, nothing here but some water, he's a water drinker, that's upstanding, you can only admire it. He's very sleepy, but he's well hydrated. There isn't a substance on earth more deserving of unmitigated approval than water. Water is good. People put it on their plants. People give it to their dogs.

No, if they found Saho passed out with a name-brand water bottle they would say, we mustn't rush to judgment here about this irreproachable water drinker. How we have let him down, let ourselves down, let down the ideals of justice. Let us pray. Let us castigate ourselves. Let us humbly resolve to do better, to be better. Who are we to judge him? How rash we were to leap to unkind assumptions. This unconscious person must have just fallen asleep half on the bed and half on the floor alongside some incidental vomit. He was probably parched, terribly parched. He must have been working very hard, could have been exercising diligently, gotten himself dehydrated, passed right out. It takes an astounding amount of mental strength to work out until you pass out. Not a man in ten thousand can do it. What determination. What focus. Perhaps he's even got a virus and here we are on the verge of adding insult to injury. The poor fellow. Why, he deserves nothing but our sympathy, our assistance, we should even elevate him, perhaps worship, no, no, a step too far, he'd be the first to say that, this humble drinker of water.

No, they'd have no case for any nascent accusations. No case whatsoever. They could prove nothing. Suspicious little rat-traitors. How dare they think their petty provocations. How could a fellow not be pushed into the occasional drink faced with an insulting attitude like that. They never gave me a chance. It's not my fault. I'll show them. This is on you, people. How do you like me now? Reflect well on what you have wrought.

You know what would go down really well right now, thought Saho, waking up in a fog. More than well. I'd even call it a craving. I'd better go visit my friends under the bridge.

# Chapter Eleven

The first day on a new job is always a mixed bag of feelings. On the one hand, you're not expected to know much of anything, so your only responsibility is to get acclimated. There will be no productivity demands, no results to show, no deadlines to meet. You can relax. Nothing can go wrong. It'll be all orientation and no work. A lot of handshakes and smiles and seeing what the people look like and judging whether they're the right sort and having them assume you know what you're doing because you're the lucky winner of the new job. You're also, in that honeymoon period, blissfully ignorant of the petty squabbles, horrendous personalities, and stupid rules that probably make it a crap place to work.

On the other hand, you feel like a bit of a putz.

Bahena felt like a bit of a putz at her first day on the new job. She had never known less about anything in her entire life, and she was the kind of person who found comfort in feeling competent.

"I know it's a lot to take in," said Juniper. "Don't sweat it."

"It is," said Bahena. "It's a lot to take in."

"You'll be fine."

Would she though? It's so easy to say you'll be fine, I'll be fine, it'll be fine, she'll be fine, they'll be fine, but obviously there were times when things and people were not fine, were far from fine. It was just a nice reassuring thing to say that came with no guarantees. It almost always elicited the subconscious objection: you don't know that. Disaster and embarrassment were as likely as anything else. It was going to take some time to learn what this gig actually entailed. Then there would be the actual communicating. Who knew what that would be like? She had considerable experience being a tactful, polite professional, but whether those skills would prove transferable was, she knew, a completely open question.

"You should relax your forehead," said Juniper.

"Oh my God, is that how the communication works?"

"No," said Juniper. "It's very wrinkly. You look so tense."

Bahena reached out and touched Juniper's shoulder.

"Oh my God, thank you," said Bahena. "For telling me, I mean."

Bahena made an obvious effort to relax her forehead muscles. She succeeded, but only by increasing the tension in other muscles elsewhere in her face, particularly around her eyes, which became fixed and bulged ever so slightly. This job was already proving to be quite the challenge, especially for low-expectations day one.

Reminding herself of her long record as a competent professional, Bahena took a deep breath, got a grip, and managed to relax the rest of her face.

"I'm a little nervous," she said. "I'll be fine."

"Of course you will!" said Juniper. "Let me show you around the rest of the office."

Juniper showed Bahena the coffee machine, the elevators, including the special elevator, and the common room and the toilets, brought her to human resources, helped her get a badge that would open literal doors for her, and introduced her to the information technology team who engaged in banter from another era where the kind of banter they engaged in was considered acceptable.

All of this orientation preamble was making Bahena more and more antsy. She could scarcely keep from grabbing Juniper by the hair and shaking her head like a jar of bubblegum balls.

"Can I see them?" she finally asked, in a tone so quiet that it conveyed screaming.

Juniper smiled.

"Why, yes," she said. "Yes, you can. Unless you'd rather see the emergency exits first or visit the stupid cafeteria and smell the institutional food smell?"

"No," screamed Bahena quietly with her eyes closed. "I'm ready."

"Right then. This way."

They went to the special elevator and took it down, down, down to the deep level where they stayed. The elevator journey took long enough for Bahena to notice uncanny windy sounds and feel like the elevator might also be haunted, or that her ghosts from her house might have trailed along for the ride. Bahena got to show her special badge to the special government security forces; she got to use her special badge to open thick sliding doors, twice. Finally, she entered a temperature-controlled room, a bit colder than a person would ideally like it, a bit more rich in oxygen. The room was empty.

Bahena looked at Juniper, who smiled and held her hand up in the universal wait-a-minute gesture.

A panel opened and in they came, as if gliding, as if jelly. They held up tiny hands and waved, issuing emanations that were perceived as sounds of ocean waves and hearts of stars and felt like hello.

# Chapter Twelve

"Canada!" exclaimed Bapa Jim. "Am I right? *Jia na da*, that's how they say it in Chinese. Big world. Everybody knows Canada."

The Special Canadian Roundtable was a rarefied affair indeed, held not in government offices – this particular roundtable was off the record, that's what made it so special – but in the executive meeting room of a luxurious private club whose every furnishing and fitting attested to the seriousness of the business of the professional world-shapers who were permitted within. Even the glass water jugs were crystal, even the water inside was like diamond water.

"Now I've got to tell you," continued Bapa Jim. "I've done my homework. I know a little something about this great land of yours. I'm not one of these fellows who comes in here and says hey, is Vancouver east or west, I can never remember, no, not me. I'm not confused about whether Saskatchewan is a province or a mythical beast roaming your magnificent woodlands. It's a beast. I'm kidding. Proud history, Canada. Proud people, proud history. Who can forget that a Canadian province cannot be sued without its consent? Can I sue you, Canadian province? No, sorry, permission denied! How great is that? That's how you stack a deck, am I right? More than one country could stand to learn a thing or two from Canadian jurisprudence, I'll tell you that for free. Who hasn't admired the traditional Canadian hostility to aboriginal land claims, or the expulsion of the Acadians, or the Council of Three Fires? How many countries can lay claim to having had on their lands a thing called the Council of Three Fires? Now, if I can lay a little of my own local vernacular on this esteemed gathering, that is just about the coolest dang thing I've ever heard of in my life and I've been around the block a couple of times. Council of Three Fires. Jesus. Can you picture it? That's a lot of fires to sit around and I can't help but believe a lot of reflection and serenity and wisdom to go with them. I've got to believe logs were added, embers were stirred, crackling was heard, smoke was smelled, stars were gazed upon. And we're just scratching the surface here. I'm just getting warmed up."

Bapa Jim refreshed his glass of water from the crystal water jug nearest his end of the table. Silently he took the temperature of the room. It was going well. People liked hearing him talk, and they liked hearing about Canada. Most of them had never even heard of the Council of Three Fires but they were glad to be hearing of it now and proud that it had happened in Canada. They liked hearing it. Badass. Council of Three Goddamned Fires.

"Do you people have any idea how many different kinds of squash have been cultivated in Canada? Of course you do, listen to me! Here I am trying to tell a group of Canadians about squash. Forgive me, gentlemen, I get carried away. It's literally dozens of kinds of squash, maybe hundreds. I'll be honest with you, I have no idea. I'm guessing. But I know it's in the multiple figures. I'd wager it is. But it doesn't take a genius to flip through some basic Canadian history and realize there are words and phrases here that are pure gold, pure maple syrup, and I think you all know exactly what I'm talking about. Paleo-Eskimos. How's that for starters? Paleo-Eskimos. The discovery of the Beothuk. The free practice of Catholicism, absolutely guaranteed. Who can forget the Canadian disappointment over the lack of a sea-water port to connect to the Yukon after the Alaskan boundary dispute of 1903? I'll say what you're all thinking: The British sold you out!"

At this the gentlemen murmured their agreement. There was at least one outright grimace and an audible "truth!"

"Hey," Bapa Jim went on, "I'm not going to lie to you, I love me some British, but those are the facts. Those are the facts and you won't hear me deny it, what's the point? Never deny a fact.

There's just no percentage in it. Unless it can buy you some time that you know how to use. Or if you can plausibly confuse the issue and there's a very good reason to do so. How about this: Never deny a fact about Canada in a room full of Canadians unless it's a fact they want denied. How about read the room before denying a fact. You get the idea. The British sold you out. Anyhow I don't blame you for being angry and if I were you, I'd still be angry today. Those wounds run deep, and I want you to know you're not alone in it. I share your disappointment. Imagine having a sea-water port to connect to the Yukon. Forty-first largest sub-national entity in the world. Nobody even lives there but just saying it out loud now makes me feel disappointed that you can't get your own access to the sea from there. An all-Canadian outlet from the Yukon to the sea, are you kidding me? The North Pacific I'm talking about, not the Arctic. I don't have to tell you nobody really cares about access to the Arctic Ocean when the Pacific is right there, and I'll tell you what else. I doubt very much that your average American citizen, by which I mean citizen of the United States, no disrespect intended to the rest of the Americas, I doubt very much he or she, no disrespect to women either, he or she understands how strange the Alaskan border really is. It all kind of makes sense from a distance, well it's that great blob of land sticking off the edge of Canada, peeking across to our old friends the Russians, from whom we bought the place to begin with – and I'll tell you, seven million was a good deal even then – but if you look closely for a minute at the southeast corner, well, you're likely to do a double take if you're paying attention. Why, it takes a sudden slippery wiggle down the coast and works its skinny little sliver halfway through British Columbia, as you'll all appreciate, almost as if it were awkwardly carved out *specifically to deny the Yukon its own access to the sea.* Sliced the Yukon coast right out of the picture. Out of nowhere. Nothing natural about that boundary. Just look at it on a map some time. I mean it's weird, isn't it? Is that just me?"

There were several rejoinders:

"It's weird."

"More than just weird."

"It's insulting is what it is."

"It's so deliberate. *So* deliberate."

"Yeah," continued Bapa Jim. "I thought so. Well, I shouldn't complain, personally, but I like to think I'm a fair-minded person and I thought that was unseemly. And I'll do you one better and say that I have a lot of respect for the genteel way you've handled it as a nation. Nobody could have blamed you for threatening violence but you didn't go that route. What the British were doing negotiating your land away in the first place could be considered something of an affront, really, if you choose to look at it that way. But not you fellows. Angry? Sure. Violent? Not on your life. Not that you wouldn't, not that you *couldn't*, but you need a proper provocation and a clear path to victory. Civilized, that's what I like to call it. That impulse toward decency is probably what led to your legalization of recreational marijuana throughout the entire nation, which I also commend you for. Why not? It's not my cup of tea personally but that's hardly the point. I know all the arguments. It makes sense. It's forward thinking. Good for you. I say go Canada. *Jia na da! Канада!*"

Bapa Jim refilled his water once again and tuned in to the room. He was doing well, still doing well. These men liked him and he liked them.

"I'll tell you something else, too," said Bapa Jim, leaning in for effect. "There are future leaders in this room. Oh yes. Future leaders of Canada. And what a Canada! Not a Canada in isolation, oh no! And not a Canada that is merely a minor party to a glorious alliance rising to meet the threat of the growing belligerence of the Combined Principalities. No! A Canada that, perhaps, in time, all in good time, is *the leading member* of that glorious partnership. Can you see that future Canada, future Canadian leaders? Can you?"

They paused; they squinted; they imagined; they had to admit they could see it.

"I am, if I may say," said Bapa Jim, "myself a humble citizen of Canada, no, not technically, not legalistically, but poetically, morally, inasmuch as I am, as are we all, are we not, citizens of empire, bound together, humbly serving to realize this great dream of a world forged in the shared wonder of our desire."

Nods and shrugs were elicited. This was special talk, high-level talk, talk with aspirations, and there were no objections.

Bapa Jim had already had similar meetings that had gone equally well in Australia, New Zealand, South Africa, and throughout Europe, amplified by the social networking of Bertie the king. He was forging an alliance of self-interested partners whose watchwords were power, duty, equality, vigilance, avarice, pugilism. If the choice was to get on board this ship that was clearly sailing or to get left behind and wave at it girlishly from the shore, well, these men knew what the thing to do was when they saw it, and they did it.

"Here's the thing," Bapa Jim explained in a new tone of voice to the assembled guests, who moved their faces into the proper concerned configurations. "Morocco. You've all heard of it. Casablanca. Rabat. Beautiful rugs. Well, something's happened. A crisis. I hate to be the one to break the news but there's no getting around it. That's why I'm here. A Moroccan crisis has occurred."

The upshot was that there was nothing for it but to intervene, which, of course, would irk the Combined Principalities. The interests of the Combined Principalities in Morocco had been officially recognized in the Recognition of Interests Act. The promise not to intervene had specifically been codified in the Paragraph on Non-Intervention.

"The Combined Principalities aren't going to like it," offered a Canadian apologetically.

"No, they won't," said Bapa Jim, smiling broadly and slapping his hand down firmly on the roundtable. "Not one little bit."

# Chapter Thirteen

It's not that easy to make a great meatloaf. You think it is, but it isn't. It's not just a giant hamburger mushed into a loaf shape. That's not going to work. That's going to fall apart on you. That's going to be dense. That's going to be dry. That's not going to have enough flavor.

Burgers aren't generally eaten on their own, without buns, ketchup, onions, mustard, pickles, lettuce, tomatoes, mayonnaise, cheese. Why aren't they eaten plain? Because they're not that interesting. They need a little help. A good meatloaf doesn't even need gravy; that's the difference. But you also can't just throw some breadcrumbs and ketchup in there and expect good results. You either have to know what you're doing or be lucky.

Bapa Jim had worked on his for years. For a long time, the results were inconsistent: sometimes it would come out well, sometimes not. But through the patient application of a scientific brand of diligence, he had eliminated much of the uncertainty. He had what he considered secrets. One of them was to grate the onions instead of chopping them. Another was to use granulated beef bouillon cubes. Another was panko breadcrumbs. Another was the mantra: mix well, press hard. Secrets. Who didn't like them? Nobody. But who could keep them?

The creation had been laid out, along with some classic sides. Bapa Jim took a moment to savor the sense of sight, savor the sense of smell, savor the sense of satisfaction. He called the family to order. They took their places around the table, but everyone seemed a little distant, not in the sense of being cold, but as if they weren't really here.

"Listen, listen, listen up," said Bapa Jim when the last scoop of mashed potato had been served, a smile spreading across his face. "I've got a new joke for you. Check it out."

Everybody smiled distractedly. Who doesn't like a joke? Good or bad, a joke is good. But who can tell them?

Saho looked up expectantly, unaware that his jaw had slackened into an unappealing gape, with some pea and potato still visible within. Bahena noticed and looked away. Matalulu noticed and convinced herself she hadn't.

"So there's two guys, right?" Bapa Jim continued, cutting his meatloaf at the same time with the side of his fork. "They're not getting along. They're arguing. One of them says to the other, you're an effete little wastrel."

Matalulu smiled as if recalling a fond memory. Bahena looked as if she could burn a hole through the table with her mind. She had told Matalulu that she had gotten a new job. Matalulu had said it was good but hadn't gotten excited, hadn't asked all sorts of questions, hadn't asked any sort of question. Thus Matalulu was left with only a vague sense that her daughter was in charge of something. A managerial thing. Important-sounding. Bit of an executive sort of thing. As usual. Things had changed only to become the same.

Saho came out of his semi-trance and closed his mouth, to everyone's unspoken half-unconscious relief.

"Everybody with me?" said Bapa Jim, who had paused expectantly to read the room, and to eat a great big bite of meatloaf, roll a bunch of peas up in some mashed potatoes, get a lot of gravy on there, and savor the taste of that package like it was the last moment before the last star in the universe blinked out and it was all black holes from here to eternity. "So anyway, the second guy..."

"Which guy?" said Matalulu.

"The effete wastrel. He objects, right? He says me? Effete? I'm the hardest man in Gdansk!"

Matalulu smiled in noncommittal fashion. She liked the sound of the word Gdansk. Wouldn't it be nice to be in Gdansk. Bahena observed Matalulu through the lens of unmet expectations. Saho watched them both spin and wobble and grow and shrink and go dark and get lighter.

"Listen, listen," said Bapa Jim. "So, the first guy says how the heck are you the hardest man in Gdansk? Only he didn't say heck. The second guy says I'll tell you why: on the coldest night of the year, I sleep with all my windows open! And the other guy, his friend, says oh, well that's not true, that's not true, I went by your flat last night and your windows were shut tight!"

What is going on, thought Saho. Bapa Jim was telling a story of some kind. He burped into his closed mouth and let it off like steam out of a little side crack.

"So the guy says," continued Bapa Jim, "listen to this, he says uh huh – and was last night the coldest night of the year then?"

Matalulu and Bahena smiled but didn't laugh because they weren't sure that was the end of the joke yet. There could have been more coming. Could have been another round of repartee, even though Bapa Jim had made an expectant face with a sort of "what do you think" motion with his fork in one hand and his knife in the other.

"That's it," said Bapa Jim, setting his utensils down and reaching for more gravy. "That's the end of the joke. He only promised about the coldest night of the year, which you can never prove except retroactively and even then he could always say he was waiting for a colder one. I'm explaining it too much now."

"Oh," said Matalulu, "I wasn't sure, sorry, I thought there could have been even more. But it doesn't need any more. That is so funny."

"That," said Bahena supportively, "is funny."

"Definitely," said Saho in order to be included.

It's a great joke, thought Bapa Jim. And was that the coldest night indeed. Got a bigger laugh in Gdansk. I am funny.

# Chapter Fourteen

Tuesday in this town was a night for lonely people, of which there were many, and cabaret die-hards, of which there were a few. Despite what Matalulu may have said when she left the house, this was not Aunt Gina's.

Matalulu had put in her time, observing other singers, listening, tuning her tendrils, absorbing, transforming her ousia. Tonight, she would take the stage for the first time. At last. She smoked extra cigarettes on the drive and repeated her own name magically. She parked and got out of the car, taking a moment to lean cinematically against the hood and enjoy the last few puffs in the night air. As she flicked the butt to the pavement and walked through the front door, she slipped her wife-and-mother persona off like a fur coat.

"Matalulu!"

"Hi, doll."

Madame Dandelion took Matalulu by the shoulders and they kissed each other's cheeks three times like the Rwandans.

"Bit of a rowdy crowd tonight, babe."

"Nothing Matalulu can't handle."

"That's my girl."

When Louis hustled up and told the friends to quit yapping because Matalulu was on in five minutes, Matalulu said: "Matalulu is ready."

She took the stage and the spotlight hit her hard. She had a microphone, a stool, and a piano player. This was it. She put her hands on her hips and squinted around the room. Not a full house. Not an empty one. The poets were here, murmuring among themselves poetically, a murmur occasionally punctuated by a shout or a hand pounding the table or some raucous laughter. Other than that, some seedy-looking salesman types and a couple of drunks. It was intimidatingly quiet as Matalulu surveyed the scene, feeling as if she were in a movie, as if the place were daring her to break the silence of no return. Charles, the piano player, kept his fingers loose and waited attentively for her signal. She smiled at him and nodded.

Her first number was Falling in Love Again. One of the drunks, meaning no harm but lacking a sense of propriety, began to shout that he was falling in love again himself. At first she ignored him, giving him time to attune himself to the mood, but he failed, he persisted. He remained poorly attuned. After his third profession of love came with a crude description of unexpurgated rudimentary fantasy, she knew this was heckling. This was a fork in the road.

"Hang on a second, Charlie," she said to the piano player, who stopped playing. Matalulu looked right at the shouty fellow, batted her eyelids, put her lips right on the microphone, and said all husky:

"Hush now, handsome. Matalulu's singing up here."

It worked, and it would always work.

Matalulu sang for four hours. She sang Rosen Aus dem Süden, she sang The Night Has a Thousand Eyes, she sang Tschi-Ki-Tin. She sang in French and in German, in English and, for the chorus of one tune, in Czech. She did an extended improvisational number in which she used not words at all but impressionistic sounds inspired by jungle flora to a light jazz accompaniment. She took a request for Is That All There Is and told Charles to play it in F Major. She kept a bottle of water on the floor and reached down to get it for an occasional sip.

It was two in the morning when she finished. The salesmen had long since left, but the drunks were going strong. They clapped with feeling. One of them was crying, and although he was predisposed to it by the small tragedies of his life, by his loneliness, by the abandonment of his dreams, by the daughter who will no longer speak to him, by the mess he'd made of his marriage, by the cheapness of his meanest decisions, by the coldness of people who were once friends, it was the power of Matalulu's voice that had nudged him on this occasion over the tearful falls. It could have been anything else, but on this night it wasn't. The poets, too, remained, and stood on the tables, clapping, saluting, bowing, and pretending to play the trumpet.

"Matalulu!" said Madame Dandelion, stepping to the microphone in her role as *conférencier* as Matalulu acknowledged her appreciators with graceful nods on her way to the bar, where Louis awaited.

"Hell of a set, babe," said Louis, handing her forty dollars in cash as Madame Dandelion ambled over to add her personal congratulations.

"Girl's a natural," said Madame Dandelion, kissing her on the cheeks three times. "Let Louis buy you a drink."

"Matalulu accepts."

"How could Louis say no?" said Louis, turning to the bartender. "Glass of champagne."

Madame Dandelion elbowed him hard in the ribs.

"Bottle of champagne," said Louis. "Not that one, not that one. Jesus. It's Tuesday, not Christmas. Yeah, that one will do just fine."

Madame Dandelion grabbed the bottle and Matalulu followed her to the dressing room, where there was bonding, encouragement, congratulations, conversation, laughter, and drinking before Matalulu excused herself. She'd had a silent idea.

She thanked Madame Dandelion, shook Louis's hand, bowed at the poets, left the room, and moved down the boardwalk to Lucky Lucca's where the bing ding doodles in the key of C and the hypnotic carpet and the mesmerizing lights welcomed her and relieved her of the capacity for thought. Space-time suspended at the slots for a singularity of nothingness until she decided to try her hand at the gaming tables and the roulette wheel like they do in the movies. She was a star now.

Everything would be glorious and celebratory and the universe would bend to her delight and curtsey at her and kiss her on the hand. It took no space-time at all before she had borrowed thirty thousand dollars from the mob and lost every last penny of it. Serious repercussions would be introducing themselves in the very near future. It took most of the drive home for her wife-and-mother persona to re-establish itself in her aura, wrapped around a new sensation of unnerving fear.

# Chapter Fifteen

Senior Complaints Investigator Pieter Beenhouwer sighed from the safety of his comfortable Utrecht office when he saw the familiar meticulous handwriting on the envelope. What is it this time, he thought in an irritated tone of mind before admonishing himself with a reminder about professionalism. Reaching for the ivory-handled letter opener he'd procured from a Nairobi street dealer on his trip-of-a-lifetime all those many years ago even though he knew ivory was bad, Beenhouwer sighed and repeated his mantra: Serenity. It hadn't been all that long since he found her letters amusing.

He unfolded the letter. The first sentence revealed it would be about tinned ham, one of his company's signature products. He furrowed his brow and read on.

Dear Senior Complaints Investigator,

We are so disappointed with this round tin of ham. The ring pull did not work; it opened about a centimeter and refused to budge any further. My husband resorted to using a knife to pry it open around the rim (rather a dangerous procedure).

It was then a matter of getting the meat out of the tin and the result was an uninviting mess as it refused to come out with ease. Needless to say we did not eat it and the whole lot went in the bin.

I regret buying this product and would not recommend it to anyone else.

I enclose some photos as evidence.

Yours sincerely,

Gina [illegible]

Pieter Beenhouwer frowned as he re-folded the letter, placed it back into its envelope, and flipped through the seven enclosed photographs, two of which were of the tinned ham *before the ring was ever pulled*, as if this Gina were expecting trouble from the get-go. The significance of Gina's inclusion of the adjective "round" in her description of the product had also not been lost on him.

Beenhouwer was only too well aware that the company had recently tried out a new shape of tin. Instead of the time-honored oval, the company was aiming to reinvigorate a stagnant tinned ham market by putting its pale pale rubbery product into a perfectly circular container. Beenhouwer had dreaded the results of this risky move because he knew better than anyone the importance of tradition to the narrow yet feisty tinned-ham demographic, and it would be he, not the geniuses up in marketing, who would bear the full brunt of their indignation.

He pulled Gina's file and reviewed some of her previous correspondence in order to gauge her state of mind as well as the appropriate response. He had his favorites.

Dear Senior Complaints Investigator,

I have just attempted to eat one of your pizzas (a Marguerita multigrain with flaxseeds) which was purchased from our local Asda last week. Because of the attractive packaging and the good in-store display, I was persuaded to try the pizza. (Photo included).

I must say it is by far and away the worst pizza I have ever tasted. The base was like cardboard; the layer of cheese was so thin that it was transparent and it had no taste whatsoever apart from a rather unpleasant saltiness.

I had always thought that your firm was a good brand and I was completely taken in by the slick marketing. I hope this feedback will persuade you to review the recipe as I cannot see how this pizza range could be successful otherwise.

Sincerely,

Gina [illegible]

"By far" or "far and away," thought Beenhouwer. One or the other, not both. Not "by far and away." Then he felt dirty for his peevishness and looked at the photographs, reliving the initial experience of processing this complaint. There was a photograph of the attractive packaging that had led Gina on the merry dance, and a photo of the admittedly good in-store display.

Then there was a photograph of the pizza product itself. A good three quarters of it was missing. The fact that so much of it had evidently been eaten was perhaps the beginning of a potential objection but would almost certainly cause more trouble than it was worth. She didn't like it. She hadn't enjoyed it. That was all that mattered. Had he denied her claim she'd only have responded that she'd eaten it in a slick hypnotic trance. Had been "taken in" by it. Had been bamboozled by the unscrupulous hucksters that populated his company. Had been temporarily deranged, like Patty Hearst. She'd have added new complaints about the resultant dyspepsia. She might've gone over the Senior Complaints Investigator's head to the Department Commander, who hated to be disturbed. Beenhouwer knew the matter would've amply redounded upon his own head. No. He had done the right thing in sending her an apology and in-kind compensation.

He shrugged and continued through the stack of correspondence. They weren't all about food. Some of them were aggressively impotent cries of nihilistic angst.

Dear Senior Complaints Investigator,

I am having great trouble accessing my account. I tried your CHAT service, but they couldn't seem to help. You keep asking me to reset my password but then it doesn't work... very frustrating. I just wanted to buy a pair of trousers.

Never mind, I'll do without!
Sincerely,
Gina [illegible]

*Who is this woman,* thought Beenhouwer. So interesting. There's the massive blank space between the exasperated throwing up of hands – I just wanted to buy a pair of trousers – and the unsatisfactory resignation of never mind, I'll do without. So much feeling in that negative space. He could almost feel her sigh, feel her sense of pointlessness. He pictured her wandering bitterly without trousers through the barren wasteland that is the human search for meaning. And why put chat in upper case letters? Did she think it was an acronym? Possible case of technophobia here, bless her. She wanted nothing from him in the end except his awareness of her suffering and his appreciation of who was responsible. The doing without harked nobly back to the deprivations of the War, a kind of salute to the stoical character of her people thanks to their unjust tribulations, and a challenge to the integrity of the merciless technocrats who forced other people to "do without." He imagined her feeling only emptiness at the steady stream of compensatory coupons appearing almost daily in her mailbox.

How to respond to this new cry for help? What were his ethical, professional, moral responsibilities? One thing that particularly troubled him were the signatures. Each message had been written with a pitiless exactitude, each individual letter perfectly formed with the tiny narrow laser focus of an eye surgeon. But the signature! It was done with such abandon that Beenhouwer could only assume it was a kind of explosive uncoiling of the tension built up by all the preceding punctiliousness. A harrowing scream of a signature. The "Gina" was a best guess, the surname a lost cause.

Could this have been our Aunt Gina, sitting in a kitchen in Wolverhampton, constantly dissatisfied, determined to leave no defect unchallenged by imperious missives sent off to remote Dutchmen?

No. There isn't the slightest indication anywhere that Aunt Gina ever lived in England, let alone somewhere in the Midlands.

No, unfortunately this was not our Aunt Gina. Merely another enticing potentiality to be crossed off the list of candidates.

Pieter Beenhouwer selected a generous three money-saving coupons for the very product she'd hated, along with his sincerely apologetic note expressing his remorse that his company's products had not met the high standards to which they aspired and his hope, his earnest hope, his Dutchman's hope, that her future experiences would result in the expected satisfaction. He knew and was at peace with the knowledge that his remorse would be appreciated and his hopes would be in vain.

# Chapter Sixteen

"So let me get this straight," said Bapa Jim. "You were only under the bridge because you were bringing hot meals to homeless people, and then they overpowered you and forced a needle into your arm."

"Basically," said Saho.

"Uh huh."

"I know it sounds crazy," said Saho.

*This is true*, thought Saho. *This is real.*

Nobody laughed.

"OK," said Bapa Jim.

Bapa Jim drove along in silence for a while, pondering tough love but opting for avoidance and hope. The phone call had been alarming, the ordeal in the emergency room harrowing. Events spoke for themselves. No further wake-up call was needed. Let the man wallow in his abject shame with dignity. And yet... a word or two, perhaps, a fatherly word.

"Just odd you never mentioned it," shrugged Bapa Jim.

"Mentioned what?"

"The whole thing where you bring hot meals to homeless people. I mean, it's fantastic, a wonderful thing to do. I could possibly have helped in some way is all."

"Ah," said Saho, working up to a feeling approaching piety. "I guess I'm a little weird about charity. Not really doing it to get credit or anything. Know what I mean? It's not about me."

"Mm hm," said Bapa Jim, nodding his understanding. "I get that."

Saho stared out of the window, watching the streetlights go by, imagining an impossibly sharp unbreakable blade protruding from the side of the car and slicing through them all one by one, leaving a trail of toppling destruction. Looked like it might rain soon. Saho hated rain. He took it personally.

"Bit ungrateful though," added Bapa Jim. "Wouldn't you say? The homeless people? Bit ungrateful? I mean I don't know if this was your first experience with this particular..."

"Bit ungrateful," confirmed Saho. "Believe me, it's the last thing I expected to happen. I was definitely as surprised as anyone."

"Yes, well, I imagine so."

"I mean," offered Saho, "these people are pretty desperate. It's hard to get into their mindset."

"Of course."

"From their point of view it stands to reason they might have been trying to do me a solid."

"How so?"

"Well, assuming they like injecting themselves with drugs..."

"They thought you might like it too."

"Exactly."

"I see. Yes, all right. And they didn't dare simply ask."

"Right, because I didn't seem the type, they wouldn't want to frighten me off."

"Yet they wanted you to have the experience."

"They thought they knew me better than I know myself."

"So that while you never would have agreed, they reckoned you'd be grateful for having been thrown into the deep end against your will, so to speak."

"Exactly. This is all just speculation, of course."

"Obviously. Obviously."

"And the benign interpretation is that they miscalculated the dosage."

"They meant well but things went south."

"That'd be the kind way to look at it."

"But you won't go back to them, naturally."

"Just let them starve because of one mistake?"

"You did nearly die."

"Let's not exaggerate."

"Your heart stopped. I'm sure that's what the doctor said."

"Well let's not be naïve, what does he charge for that?"

"But..."

"No, of course you're right. I won't go back after this."

It did start to rain. Sooner even than it looked like it might. They were nearly back at the house and it was nearly dinner time.

"The doctor did mention something else a bit interesting," said Bapa Jim, keeping his eyes with steely focus on the road.

Saho's internal alarm went off, the one that always felt somber, a death knell, right in the middle of his chest.

"What's that?" he responded tightly.

"Just something about there being more than just the one needle mark. I don't remember it exactly, but wasn't it something like that? Something about plenty of them, and not all of them fresh? Am I remembering that correctly?"

"No, I don't remember anything like that."

"Ah."

"Maybe he was confused by the little marks where I got vaccinated, I don't know."

"Yes, probably. Or maybe he saw some moles or freckles and thought they were old needle marks. With all the things they see, doctors must get very confused about what it all means."

*Is the old man mocking me*, wondered Saho.

"Well it's busy in there and they do see a lot of junkies, so..."

"They probably make a lot of quick assumptions."

"Exactly."

"Unfair assumptions."

"I mean hey," said Saho, "they do a great job, I'm not knocking them, but I mean, I guess I'd know if I had lots of old needle marks!"

"Seems reasonable. Unless those insane homeless jabbing maniacs have done this to you before, of course. Unless you blacked out from it and just had no memory of it."

"Could be," said Saho, open to all theories except the unspoken one. "Could be that too, I guess. I mean I don't remember blacking out or forgetting anything."

"Yes, well, how could you? Almost by definition."

"Good point."

Bapa Jim parked the car. Saho by now had achieved belief in the story about the homeless people overpowering him and sticking needles into his arm out of misplaced beneficence or hostility. If he were to become old one day, it is very likely that he'd reach into his memory and pull it out, indistinguishable from the real, both believable and believed, he'd pull out the story of that time he brought some hot food to some homeless people and they ungratefully attacked him in order to jab him with a needle. Vengeful. Unhinged. Cruel. Or then again merely misguided, distorted. If anyone found it hard to believe, he'd swear up and down and resentfully add details.

"Umbrella?" offered Bapa Jim, unbuckling his seat belt.

"Nah," said Saho, opening his door and lurching unsteadily toward the house. "I hate the rain."

# Chapter Seventeen

"OK, OK, I get it," said Bahena. "Let me try it again real quick."

It was time for Bahena to start getting to know the clients. She was blindfolded – a temporary measure that supposedly made the initial communications easier. Eventually – pretty soon – it would no longer be necessary; she'd just be able to snap into the right frame of mind automatically. At first, however, the idea was that the visual signal deprivation had a mind-opening effect, instantly privileging other senses that normally took a back seat. The disorientation was also supposed to be a positive.

"It puts you in pairing mode," Juniper had explained. "At first we used a machine but eventually we learned we didn't need it."

Bahena had no optimism about any of this working, and a ready-made assumption that it would be her own fault. She would not be sensitive enough. She would not be clever enough or open enough. She wouldn't be able to let go and ride the omni-connecting tendrils of the all-feeling universe like a perfectly adaptive super surfer. The signals would be there but she'd fail to recognize them. She'd be deaf to it. She'd be a real let-down. The clients would reject her. She'd leave without her dignity. She'd leave without her job.

However, Bahena's fears proved unfounded. Indeed, almost immediately she was practically overwhelmed with sensations, as if her brain were in a wind tunnel of neuronal impulses. You couldn't miss it. You didn't have to be special or exquisitely sensitive. There was no mistaking it. It sat her back in her chair as if she'd been shoved into it by a firehose.

"OK," she said, feeling like she'd just been launched in a rocket and needed to weather the G forces for a while. What began as a shattering deluge of chaotic waves soon took on decipherable shapes. It no longer felt like an assault. She had not exploded or gone psychotic. She was not drooling.

"You're pairing," said Juniper. "Stick with it."

Bahena wouldn't have known how to disengage anyway at that point, nor did she want to. It was a pleasant sensation, confusing but pleasant. None of it was like words but it had patterns and intelligence. When she tried to send thoughts and feelings the other way, that is to say when she had thoughts and feelings, she felt like they were received, she felt she was getting responses. This was a two-way flow. It was less that she was being bombarded with something and more that she had joined something, rode it, was it. She wasn't afraid. There was no sense of threat. It was all somehow affirming, devoid of the defensive posturing that normally characterized all work-related communications. She had never felt this combination of honesty and serenity. She trusted and felt trusted.

"This is good," she said. "I like this."

She felt a query and nodded her assent, murmuring the word "yes" unnecessarily. Speaking to Juniper was the difficult bit now, she had to break the trance, but getting back in was smooth and easy.

"They're going to teach me something," she said. "This sounds strange, but I think it's about a Rubik's cube. You have one. I'm sure you have one."

"Yeah, I tried this one too, hang on."

Juniper went to the supply closet, fetched one of several Rubik's cubes from a shelf, and handed it to Bahena. Bahena held the cube and took a deep breath.

"OK," she said, unnecessarily. First, she twisted it all up in random directions. More, came the response she felt; she twisted it more. Next, placing her index finger on the top right up-facing corner, she easily stopped thinking. After a few seconds, she nodded confidently.

"It's green," she said, and smiled. She knew it as surely as if she wasn't blindfolded at all.

A confirming sensation urged her to take the next step.

"All right, all right," murmured Bahena. Honestly, she thought, I'm already amazed to have done this much. But OK. Here we go. Good, came the encouraging response in her feelings.

She began turning and rotating the sections of the cube, slowly at first, but picking up speed until her fingers were working more nimbly than they ever had at anything. From start to finish it was less than thirty seconds before she had solved the puzzle, and she knew it was successful, knew it for sure, even before she took the blindfold off.

"Wow," she said. "That's crazy."

"Right?" said Juniper. "OK, true confessions? I tried at least a hundred times and could not pick it up. I'm like blocked. I'm really proud of you. I think they like you. I always felt like they were just messing with me to be honest. I don't know. I think they find me off-putting."

"Well, I can't imagine why."

"You better say that! Do you want to take a break?"

"Not really, I'd like to keep going. All right you guys, what are we going to tune into next? Really? No, no, I've never played..."

# Chapter Eighteen

"I didn't know you liked chess," Bapa Jim said to his daughter, trying not to sound surprised, leaving out the part where he didn't think she was smart enough or interesting enough for the game. Bapa Jim was preoccupied with justifying the seizure of a couple of Moroccan ports, perhaps by planting a false news story about some Chaouyas tribesmen butchering a number of Frenchmen. He smiled at the thought of the Combined Principalities' reaction to the provocation before remembering that his spirits were low thanks to his son having almost died as a result of being a relentless screw-up. He almost felt there must be something to say or do but, of course, there was nothing. Could better parenting have helped at some point? Well. The boy had every opportunity. He had the brains. He'd been loved. He was a fine-looking boy. Look at Bahena. Same parents. Explain that. Had to be an extra-parental factor. Some invisible connection had snapped somewhere, been pulled out, got chewed on, that's all. Something had gone haywire. It was nobody's fault. Life is very difficult and things do go wrong.

Bahena had come by for a visit because she had heard about Saho's misadventure from Matalulu and was concerned for her brother. Bapa Jim hadn't told her, hadn't told Matalulu either, because it wasn't the sort of story he liked to tell or wanted anybody to hear. But Matalulu had understood that something had happened, and between the lies that Saho told her and the things Bapa Jim did not say, she had pieced together a close representation of the truth. She'd rung Bahena and given it to her on the sly. The family had come together, but nobody had said a word about it. That would be grotesquely direct and would cause an unacceptable awkwardness. Although they were together, Saho was in a world apart, his brain stimulated by imprisoned xenon and neon atoms in little cells tortured by electrodes into producing a lifelike representation of a real-time baseball game, the overall effect causing his mouth to hang slightly agape. He was dimly suspicious that the gathering around him had something to do with his troubles. The awareness was further dimmed by his obstinate yet subconscious refusal to accept that anyone could possibly have known anything about his secretive activities at all. How dare they come here. How dare they know anything. The air was thick with supercilious forbearance.

"I've only recently taken up the game," said Bahena. "My new clients have been teaching me. They're teaching me all sorts of things."

*Clients*, half-thought Bapa Jim who had half been listening. It reminded him that Bahena had lost a job recently or something, possibly just gotten one, maybe struck out on her own somehow, he was surely supposed to know this. Clients. The sort of word people who don't have jobs use. Play it cool, figure it out on the fly.

"Clients," he said. "Jobs. Work. Am I right?"

Bahena was a good daughter who refrained from rolling her eyes.

"Right you are," she said.

*Poor thing*, thought Bapa Jim. I really hope she finds something suitable unless she already has. She probably will or won't or has or hasn't. It's not our fault. She's got the tools. She's been loved. There's only so much and then it's whatever it is. Children, am I right? They'll go their own way, ultimately. They'll live their lives, not yours. Way of the world. Let go and get on.

"Anyway, maybe I can offer the odd tip here and there," said Bapa Jim, who fancied himself a bit of a dab hand at the game of kings. "I guess I've picked up a thing or two in my day. Control the center, and if you can't do that, get things going on the flank!"

Matalulu appeared from the kitchen, bearing celery and carrot sticks, salsa and tortilla crisps, barbecued chicken wings.

"Thank you, darling," said Bapa Jim, adding as he moved his piece: "Queen to e2." Naming the square made him feel pleasantly smug. Bet Bahena didn't know the name of the square. I won't point it out. She'll pick it up naturally over time.

"*De nada*," said Matalulu, placing an affectionate maternal hand momentarily on Saho's shoulder.

Snacking ensued. The game progressed.

"In the gap!" shouted Saho suddenly, none of the words achieving true clarity, awkwardly, as if Frankenstein's monster were trying to dance. "Double! Two runs in!"

"You all right over there, Saho?" asked Bahena.

"Yes," said Saho defensively. *Why on earth*, he thought, *would you ask me such a thing?* There is no official reason!

"I mean we got chicken wings here," she said.

*Oh*, thought Saho. Chicken wings. His long arm reached over and behind from his comfortable couch and snatched one in a way that was just short of impossible.

"Mmmm," he said, and Matalulu felt a measure of comfort. One does what one can, does one not? They've been fed, they've been loved. There's always been a roof. A floor. A bed. Walls. Running water.

The game progressed to the late stages. Bapa Jim offered more and more advice as he fell further and further behind. Bahena took his pawn on b2 with her rook, allowing him to capture back with his knight on a4. A whole rook, for the price of a pawn. Poor Bahena, thought Bapa Jim. Just not the brightest bulb in the scissor factory drawer.

"I don't think you want to do that," he said, and to his credit he tried not to sound patronizing. "You can take it back if you like. No big deal – but you owe me one!"

"Hmmm no, I'm good."

"Are you sure?"

"Pretty sure."

"Well OK, if you're sure."

The problem then dawned on him. Her pawns on the c file now could not be stopped. She had given up a rook but gained one, possibly two queens if it came to that.

"That's actually... not so bad for you," he said.

"Yes," she said, and to her credit she tried not to sound smug. "Not so bad."

Two moves later, he resigned. How had she done it? Was it luck? She wasn't the sort, and yet she seemed quite sure. Some sort of fluke. Well, thought Bapa Jim, I'll have to pay more attention. I've got other chess matches on my mind. Didn't see it coming though. *What a slip-up.*

Bahena went home after placing a sisterly hand on Saho's shoulder. Bapa Jim slapped him on the same shoulder before going to the bathroom. Matalulu had squeezed that shoulder on one of her trips to the kitchen. All this shoulder touching gave Saho frightening half-formed feelings that people might know all about him, might see him in ugly nakedness, he might be as plain as day, a pathetic figure, a deluded fool, but no: impossible.

Presently Matalulu excused herself; she had to go visit Aunt Gina, who remained unwell. The baseball team won despite some poor relief pitching but Saho missed it; he had fallen asleep on the couch.

Bapa Jim sighed. He picked up the phone and notified the influence network about a massacre in Morocco. It seems some Chaouyas tribesmen had murdered between fifty and a hundred Frenchmen in a challenge to European authority that could not be ignored. The Combined Principalities might not like French intervention, but something would have to be done. France would have to respond. May I suggest seizing a couple of ports? There would be no choice but to do something once it hit the newspapers.

# Chapter Nineteen

The young sultan was riding his bicycle joyously near the Bou Regreg river near Rabat. He tried riding with no hands. Whoa, whoa, whoa! It got wobbly, so he grasped the handlebars once again and smiled. He tried a wheelie: so-so! He tried again: a little better. He would get it one day. He could feel it. One day soon.

One of his aides came running up to him waving a newspaper.

"Your majesty!" the man cried. "Your majesty!"

His majesty tried drifting into a sharp turn. Not bad, not bad! Quite a bit of dust kicked up!

"Yes, yes, what is it?" said the Sultan, annoyed at the interruption but resigned to dealing with important business at inconvenient times.

"You must see this! It's in all the European papers!"

The aide thrust a copy of *Le Figaro* into the Sultan's hands. A banner headline blared news of how some Chaouyas tribesmen had massacred a substantial pile of Frenchmen for unclear motives attributed to generalized hostility toward Europe.

"Chaouyas tribesmen?" muttered the Sultan, frowning at the page. "Pile of Frenchmen? Massacre?"

"Yep," said the aide.

"This is horse shit, right?" said the Sultan.

"Yep," said the aide.

"Welp," said the Sultan. "They'll be coming, then."

"Yep," said the aide.

The Sultan thought for a moment and rang the bell on his new bike absent-mindedly. What a lovely tone it had. Marvelous.

"Not to worry," he said, smiling. "It's not us they're really after. Take this newspaper and put it by the toilet where it can do some good."

"Yes, your majesty!"

And that is the story of the Sultan and his new bicycle.

# Chapter Twenty

Things were slow at the old Broken Goose and Big Tony the mobster stood towering over Matalulu at the bar with his arms folded, an expectant look on his face.

Not sure what to do and wanting to buy time, Matalulu tried simply not looking at him so that maybe he would go away or in some way would not really have ever been there at all. She stubbornly looked down at the umbrella in her drink, imagining a tiny person in a tiny boat under it in the rain, a tiny person wondering about the round enclosure, wondering about how to get out, about how they got there in the first place, about the giant ice cubes, about what kind of crazy lake this was, about where was the land, about why didn't anything make sense. She was trying to convince herself that thirty thousand dollars wasn't that much money. The best way to get thirty thousand dollars not to be that much money was to think of much larger amounts of money: sixty thousand dollars, for example; one hundred and seventy thousand dollars; five hundred and twenty-two thousand dollars. Forty billion dollars. Thirty trillion dollars. So, she thought up figures of that size or better quite dreamily for a little while, and by the time she alighted back on the figure of thirty thousand dollars, it seemed downright paltry.

Another way of getting thirty thousand dollars not to be so much money was to think of it over time. Thirty thousand dollars over a decent lifetime was perhaps a dollar a day, even less if you were in for a particularly good innings. Another thing that could be done was to imagine rich people who wouldn't get out of bed for less than forty thousand dollars, who wouldn't notice if thirty thousand dollars fell through a hole in their pocket, who spent that much on wine every single month, who would use thirty thousand dollars to wipe their bottoms. Matalulu could almost begin to feel contempt for thirty thousand measly chickenshit dollars.

There were two obvious problems with the maintenance of this contempt that hardly need to be spelled out. First, unlike the distracting fantasies in her head, the money she'd lost was as real as money gets, which is to say not that real, but robustly sustained by a widely agreed-upon belief system. Second, Big Tony wasn't in the mood for any nonsense.

Matalulu looked up at him and affected nonchalance.

"Thanks for coming," she said, as if she had invited him. "How'd you like the show?"

"I thought you were good," said Tony. "Real good. Most of the rest of it, I'll be honest with you. I could take it or leave it."

"So," said Matalulu. "You want your money. Or what – you'll kill me?"

"Why you want to rush right into talking about killing people? Nobody said anything about killing anybody."

"Because that's mob stuff," said Matalulu, poking him in the chest with her pointy finger. "Money and killing people. Everybody knows that."

"Yeah?"

"Yeah."

"You want my advice? A lot of stuff everybody knows just ain't so."

"You want *my* advice?" said Matalulu, poking him again. "You shouldn't kill people."

"Philosophically? Sometimes it's gotta be done," said Tony, looking Matalulu steadily in the eye while pushing her pokey finger off of his chest. "It's never a happy thing. Some guys like it."

"And you?"

"I do what I have to."

"Even when it's not what you want to do?"

"Have to means have to."

"A lot of people think they have to do a lot of things they don't have to do."

"Hey, bartender," said Tony. "Another one of these umbrella drinks for the lady. And give me a Cutty and water."

"Who said you could buy me a drink?"

"You don't have to drink it."

"If I did," said Matalulu, "I wouldn't."

The bartender delivered the drinks and Matalulu took hers in hand.

"Cheers," she said.

"To Matalulu," said Tony.

"To Matalulu."

They clinked glasses.

"I got nothing against you personally," said Tony. "I'll be honest with you: I like you. I wish you well. I really do. Plus, you're a hell of a singer and you've got the panache. Know what I'm saying?"

"Matalulu sings like hell with panache."

"That's right. But that doesn't change the basics."

"Matalulu owes money to the mob."

"Yes, she does."

"Come on," said Matalulu. "What do you care?"

"I don't follow."

"Simple. Thirty thou? Pfft. Who gets worked up over that? It's hardly a million and it didn't come out of your personal pocket. Make the adult move. Write it off."

"You need to take this more seriously."

"That sounds like a threat."

"Now you're listening. I can give you a week. One week from today, right here, you need to give me forty thousand dollars. Those are the facts."

"Forty? It's thirty."

"Interest."

"How is Matalulu going to do that?"

"That's your business."

"Why don't you give me a little more money?"

"What for?"

"Roulette."

"You want a shovel with that? I mean while you're digging yourself deeper?"

"You got a better idea?"

"Yeah. Not doing that."

"You want your money back, right? Matalulu feels lucky."

Big Tony sighed. Reluctantly he agreed to the proposition with an offhand comment about whose funeral it was. Before the night was out, Matalulu lost all the money at the roulette wheel and owed a hundred and twenty thousand dollars to the mob. Plus interest.

The last thing she saw before heading out the back door in some haste was Big Tony across the room, looking right at her. Shaking his head.

# Chapter Twenty-One

At a recent conference in Leipzig on the theme of Who Was Aunt Gina, one provocative session argued that Aunt Gina was one of the many interconnected women involved in the ownership of nightclubs in London whose deaths within months of each other were ruled as accidents or suicides. The scholars vested in this theory acknowledged that they were unable to offer irrefutable proof. The possibility cannot, however, be ruled out. Extant descriptions are roughly similar to other known descriptions and we do know that some of these women were aunties, coincidentally enough. Furthermore, one of them, intriguingly as you please, was called Gina X.

Gina X was living what the gossip rags called "the gay life," by which they meant "dancing at midnight... drinks at dawn." Club Personal Touch, the place she owned, was by then beginning to get a bad reputation for selling intoxicating liquors outside of approved hours and for attracting a dubious clientele. Eventually, official proceedings were started against the establishment and within three months it had officially been struck off: its license to do business was revoked without appeal.

Despite the law's best attempts, the club did not actually close. Instead, it changed names and was now called Angel Baby Blue. The Chief Inspector went in there personally and found it unabashedly doing business, complete with drinking and dancing. The inspector was outraged and had the manager, a small man called Max with enormous hands, hauled in front of a judge, where he was fined an insignificant amount of money. We will hear more about Max shortly.

Around that time the Angel Baby Blue was rumored to be the subject of negotiations for a change in ownership. Gina had been living with an accountant, a man who knew how to make bad money look good. Her close friends later reported that Gina would alternate between periods of almost hysterical exuberance contrasting with days at a time when she was gripped with an intense paranoia where she refused to go outside at all.

Paranoia isn't always irrational. There had been a lot of death in the local nightclub scene around that time, especially involving women who owned or managed clubs. Gina's friend Ruth, who managed a nearby club called Pearls, was given the death penalty and executed after she shot and killed her lover, a shady and abusive character who most people reckoned had gotten exactly what he had coming. After Ruth was hanged, her young colleague Linda took over the management of Pearls. Ruth had hired Linda as a hostess when she was only seventeen, a mousy little schoolgirl with hopes and dreams that quickly soured in the hardscrabble realities of the London night life. Within six weeks Linda was dead too, a suicide they said. Pills. She was found fully clothed in her unlocked apartment. The cops didn't seem that interested in the debts she had accumulated to some notorious gangster types, nor in her reluctant relationship with an equally notorious and abusive conman.

A few days before Linda bought the farm, one of her friends, an ex-showgirl called Janet was found dead at the home she shared with her husband, a Queen's Counsel with ties to MI6. She was found in bed cuddled up to her pet kitten, Tiddlywinks. The coroner called it barbituric poisoning and mentioned conflicting evidence but said he was "obliged" to call it self-administered – an interesting choice of words. Two weeks later, the QC husband was also found dead: barbituric poisoning.

The next death was a big shot in the nightclub world, one Esmerelda Birdsong, who started out as a promising young starlet and ended up owning four of the busiest clubs in London. One night a couple of weeks after Linda and Janet died, Esmerelda went home with one of her hostesses, a girl called Valerie, and two unspecified men. They partied there until dawn. Some time later that morning, the men were gone and

Valerie and Esmerelda were found unconscious, the apartment full of gas. Valerie was dead at the scene, but Esmerelda was still alive and taken to a hospital. She was questioned but was only able to murmur incoherently before she, too, succumbed. The coroner blamed the gas; the Gas Board said the amount of gas was insufficient to have created dangerous conditions. The coroner stuck to his guns.

Following Esmerelda's death, her biggest club fell into the hands of a Satanist sex-party host and blackmail artist who turned it into a gambling den frequented by gangland criminals, politicians, intelligence agents, and members of the royal family.

Another nightclub hostess, this one called Pamela, described by her friends as "the gayest of us all" thanks to her unwavering commitment to dancing until dawn in drinking establishments, was found blue in her own gas-filled apartment around this same time period, having made sure her pet budgies were safely locked in the bathroom. An unsympathetic newspaper piece appeared at this point noting that the nightclub hostess's life was one of debauchery and desperation. These young ladies were paid next to nothing, said the article, making them entirely dependent upon tips from the mostly male customers who didn't give up their money for nothing. According to unnamed sources, the girls were chosen for "their good looks and their light-hearted view on virtue."

Regardless of what we may surmise about the causes of these deaths, we can understand how our Gina X might have felt a little bit on edge. Max, the manager of Angel Baby Blue, was an intriguing character who had a previous career smuggling weapons in used cars to wherever the CIA wanted weapons to go. Max ended up decapitated with his legs chopped off. His head was found in one box, his legs in another a few miles away. The rest of him – his torso, as it were, with his hands still tied behind his back – was put in a third box and tossed out of a single-engine Cessna into the sea.

As for Gina, her story unfortunately does not have a happy ending, but she did have an interesting demise. She was found sitting on a plush chair in a black evening gown and a standard lamp lying near her body. A bottle of sleeping pills was found on a side table and bagged as evidence. The pathologist noted bruises on her knuckles consistent with having struck something with force. She had apparently become entangled with the cord of the floor lamp, to which marks on her wrist and neck were attributed.

The pathologist noted that the amount of Seconal in her body was by no means enough to kill her, and furthermore insisted that the lamp's cord had certainly not asphyxiated her. What, then, had happened? He offered a conjectural scenario in which Gina came home, took a non-lethal dose of sleeping pills, and proceeded to fall into a chair in such a way that a lamp cord had gotten wrapped around her neck and wrists in a non-lethal manner. Pressed once again by the coroner for the cause of death, the pathologist – presumably shrugging in a sheepish manner – said it must have been the combination of the two otherwise non-lethal events. He said there was nothing to suggest suicide, leaving unfortunate accident as his official conclusion. The Angel Baby Blue continued on, shifting its focus from dancing to being a blackmail-oriented Satanist gambling sex club for mob-connected politicians working for the intelligence agencies.

Were this in fact the very same Aunt Gina of our particular interest, it would, of course, raise certain questions, in particular about timing. How, for example, could she have figured in Matalulu's life long after her tragic demise? That would perhaps be the greatest mystery in a puzzle already teeming with them. But we shall prefer to remember this Gina as her friends did, on her last night alive, dancing as the band played Memories Are Made of This, throwing a coin into the fountain pool guarded by a blue plaster angel, and leaving with a wave of her hand and the promise: "See you tomorrow."

# Chapter Twenty-Two

Saho was still suffering from the after-effects of having to make up elaborate stories for the benefit of people whose business it wasn't. He reckoned his little tale about uninvited injections had held up all right, but for whatever reason it didn't prevent a kind of disconsolate aura from settling around him like a malarial mist. Going out to get into humiliating trouble was his natural inclination, but he just couldn't work up the necessary spiritual energy to take the first step.

Therefore he stayed in his room, lying on his bed. This was in any case what Bapa Jim had advised him to do, for as long as necessary. Rest. Recover. Take it easy for a while.

He poked around on his phone for a long time, watching videos of men having face-slapping contests and looking at some photos in the endless series of extremely similar selfies posted constantly by one of his social media friends he had never met. He sent her an approving direct message, thought of her fleetingly as his girlfriend, just a sort-of girlfriend but, of course, not really, and then watched a long series of videos featuring drivers receiving instant karma for their aggressive driving behaviors. Eventually, however, his phone felt hot in his hands, his arms felt weak, and he closed his eyes.

Saho was hiking in what appeared to be the Berkshire foothills or some similar modest mountain range. It must have been in the fall because everything was Froot Loops colors. He was with Sonny, a former child with little hopes and dreams who had grown up to be a complete scumbag as a result of circumstances and choices. Sonny was his comparison friend, the fellow you were at least not as bad as. Saho and Sonny trembled and were afraid down below but laughed on top.

Saho felt irritated because it was hot and he had a winter coat on and no shoes. He took off his coat but then he had to carry it. Finally, he threw it into some bushes but then felt bad about that. Then he couldn't find it again to reclaim it. Now he had no coat and it wasn't hot and he felt bad about everything, and the ground was covered in sharp sticks. Why hadn't he put shoes on?

Sonny had a hip flask and kept drinking from it. He'd offer it to Saho but when he held it out it was dripping with Sonny's saliva, so much so that it was implausible. It was an entire hip flask full of Sonny's saliva and it dripped everywhere. Saho didn't question it, he merely recoiled. Sonny grinned, leered, wobbled, pulled his zipper down, got his pecker out, and let loose with a stream of urine so profound that it threatened to fill up the valley around them.

Saho became alarmed as it became clear that the urine level was rising and that the whole mountain had become unpleasant, even the sky had become dark and the environment had taken on aspects of sewage and revenge.

"We have to get higher," he said to Sonny, indicating with his nose the path up the mountain.

"Sounds good to me!" shouted Sonny, gleefully misinterpreting everything and finally zipping up his trousers.

Saho set off on the path, not caring if Sonny followed. Sonny was gone now and Saho topped the rise and thought he was at the peak but it was a false peak; as he went a little bit further another peak was revealed. He made that one. Again, it was false and he continued in this vein until finally he understood he was at the true summit but it was inside a diner. There was music. Was it his mother singing? It sounded like his mother singing when he was little, over the sound of a vacuum cleaner, and Saho shot things out of his Six Finger, an ingenious fake-finger toy that shot things.

Saho sat down in a booth, but a man put his hand on his shoulder and said in a velvety voice I'm sorry but that's my booth. Saho looked up and it was Johnny Mathis, Columbia

Records' most experienced performer and the originator of the greatest hits album concept.

"You're welcome to join me," said Johnny Mathis. "I'm having the champagne."

Johnny Mathis was a little bit drunk.

"I'm not a mean drunk," said Johnny Mathis, patting Saho's shoulder reassuringly. "I wanted to be a jazz singer. Like Sarah Vaughan, or Ella. That's how I started."

"Sooooo…"

"Not at all. Things went a different way, but, well, I can't complain."

"The Twelfth of Never."

"I'll tell you a secret. I hated that song."

"Me too."

"You? Really? Why?"

"Just not my style."

"I thought it was very repetitious. Nothing happened in it. It went nowhere."

Saho pointed his Six Finger at the iconic stylist and fired the fragmentation bomb into his chest.

Johnny Mathis picked up the two pieces of the fragmentation bomb and examined them.

"May I?"

"Sure." Saho handed over the Six Finger for a Mathis inspection.

Johnny Mathis scrawled a message on a small piece of paper, tucked it into the message missile, and fired it at Saho's chest. Saho picked up the message missile and extracted the message after coaxing it forward with his fingernail. Saho unrolled it and read it out loud:

"Nancy Reagan."

"I was close friends with the First Lady," said Johnny Mathis. "I was a mess and she confronted me. She got me into rehab."

*Is that what this is about,* thought Saho. Some crummy little trick to get me into rehab? The nerve. I had respect for legendary recording artist Johnny Mathis until this moment. The ladies were all crazy for him. OK. I had girlfriends too. I'm not nothing in the girlfriend department myself.

Saho pointed the Six Finger at the singer and hit him in the chest with the cap bomb. When the smoke cleared, the velvet-voiced crooner was gone, and who was sitting there in his place but Sonny the illustrious dirtball and erstwhile child. Sonny grinned and popped three powerful opioids into his mouth, washing it down with a sugary fizz drink that made you notice how brown his teeth were. Saho virtuously popped only one of the pills.

At least I'm not as bad as Sonny, he thought. At that moment, unbeknownst to him, in real life, his father found him on the floor, covered him with a blanket, turned around, and padded off to bed. He would or wouldn't sort himself out and that would be that. It would be what it was.

# Chapter Twenty-Three

When Bahena and Saho were small, immature, likable people of single-digit years, Saho was always smaller, less mature, and more likable. Matalulu doted on him. Bapa Jim bounced him on his knee. Bahena once dropped a plate and broke it. It wasn't carelessness so much as it was a slippery dish with lots of gravy on it. She had only been trying to help, had only been trying to be a good child, a child who helped with the dishes by bringing them from the table to the sink.

The plate shattered on the kitchen floor.

Bahena remembers standing there crying. Shocked, ashamed, frightened. Far from receiving sympathy for the obvious trauma she had endured, she received only merciless opprobrium. She was a silly girl, air-headed and clumsy, said her mother in a moment a therapist might say was cruel projection. She needed to pay attention to what she was doing, advised her father who had yet to master kindliness. Never mind the gravy, never mind the excuses. Just apologize and clean up the mess. Next time try to be less stupid. We may take this out of your allowance. The specter of her mother's wooden spoon whispered around the darkest parts of Bahena's psyche, subconsciously torturing the same bits of hindbrain responsible for the terror of the shadow creatures that lived in the basement, the ones she called jackies. She might be chased into the basement, alone with the jackies who would pull her into the recesses. She felt caught between jackies and wooden spoons.

Her mother never threatened her with the wooden spoon. She didn't have to. Not after it had been used that one time for the candy-stealing incident.

Later on during the day of the shattered plate, Saho went flying along the upstairs hallway at top speed chasing Bahena during a game of Chase Bahena. She shrieked and ran into her room. Saho leapt feet first at the bedroom door in an attempt to bash it open before she could close it. The attempt failed; Bahena had fully closed the door and it had latched. The result was that Saho's momentum carried him into a crash and his foot went straight through the outer layer of the cheap, hollow plywood door.

Did their mother chastise Saho? Did their father call him a silly, air-headed, clumsy boy? Did he need to pay attention to what he was doing? Did he need to forget all about making excuses and take a little responsibility? Were there threats to take the damage out of his allowance? Did they worry that, had he succeeded in slamming the door back open, it might have smashed into Bahena and injured her? Did he get bashed about with wooden spoons and pulled into dark recesses by slithery jackies?

Far from it! Matalulu and Bapa Jim raced upstairs to see if Saho was all right. Had he damaged his little foot? His precious ankle? His delicate knees? They cuddled him, told him not to worry, gave him a playful pat on the head. Hell of a kick you've got there, ace. Jeez, easy on the door there, Hercules. The hole never did get fixed. They just put a picture over it and the family lived with it for years.

Saho also got more praise for doing well in school, whereas Bahena could come home top of the...

OK, came the sensations. *Enough*, said the vibrations. *We get it already.*

This was not the sympathetic response Bahena had been hoping for when she forgot herself and let loose with the bitter recollections from her childhood. Was that the sensation of her clients rolling their eye-equivalents? Was that a sarcastic boo hoo?

A pause in communications. Patience? A kind of waiting?

You might have a shred of sympathy, felt Bahena. It wouldn't kill you.

Another pause.

Fine. Be that way. Be just like them. Why be any different? Why shouldn't the entire universe be against me? Why not...

The clients flooded her over the course of perhaps three long seconds with a sense bomb constructed of humanity at its most depraved, from a condensed history of everywhere, things that happen, even to children, that are not amusing to recount, leaving her literally on her knees, her mind figuratively broken into shards of pure scream.

"OK," she eventually said. "Maybe I was up my own bum a little bit there."

Then a warm feeling and a communication, like tiny fly wings fluttering directly in her brain, saying the vibrational equivalent of:

"Still, we'd have to admit. Not cool of them. Unfair."

"Not cool," said Bahena. "Thank you. That's all I'm saying. Not cool."

An unsettling feeling with ropes around it that burned your hands because you were sliding down too fast out of control soon had Bahena sitting up in bed in a panic because she wasn't at work in the special room with her clients at all. She was home, in the house that was maybe haunted, and there were strange scratching sounds coming from the wall, as if from inside the wall, as if something was trying to get out. All things considered it couldn't be said that it would be impossible for the clients to communicate with her over this distance, which made Bahena feel like, hey, wait a minute, I don't even have to go to the office at all, I could telecommute. A cold clay feeling with moths and spider webs on the face said to her *work through it, do this, be you.* Out of the corner of her eye she saw, or thought she saw, an apparition, a woman dressed all in white but fleeting, and Bahena could see right through her. But when she turned her head directly at the white woman to get a better look, she wasn't there anymore and it might have been just the light from the headlights of a passing car outside. *Classic*, thought Bahena, staying cool. A photograph in a frame on her nightstand, a picture of her as a child on a swing with her smiling father pushing her fell over, arguably because she might've hit the nightstand with her elbow turning to see the woman in white. She felt cold and thought of the jackies that lived in her basement. They were coming up the stairs. They were going to drag her down into the back of the basement by the boiler. There was no imagining what would happen after that. There was no after that. That would be it.

*Girl you've got issues* said a wiggling sensation from the clients. So she was at work after all, in the special room. She had simply gotten disoriented and self-involved.

"Do you guys believe in ghosts?" she thought-said.

"No," said the clients. "But do watch out for basement jackies."

Please don't joke about that, thought Bahena, and the clients tried not to show that they thought it was pretty funny. The truth was they enjoyed getting to know her. They even took an interest in her parents.

# Chapter Twenty-Four

Bapa Jim sat in the sauna with the president of France, remarking on what a jolly fellow old Bertie was and how fine it was to be all together in some sort of great adventure. They had just finished a rousing game of tennis. Whether Bapa Jim had let the president win is a question to which we may never have a reliable answer.

"So!" said the president in flawless English. "I have beaten you!"

"Yes," said Bapa Jim. "Soundly."

"Soundly!" repeated the French president robustly, his rosy jowls reverberating and sweaty.

"*Vive la France!*" shouted Bapa Jim.

"*Vive la France!*"

The men sighed in unison, perhaps reflecting on the glory of France, but each lost in his own momentary private thoughts.

"I am also out-sweating you!" declared the French president, looking at the rivulets coursing down his flabby pectorals and arms.

"It appears that you are!" agreed a sweaty but not excessively sweaty and comparatively toned Bapa Jim, and if he had taken offense at the unseemly competitiveness, he did not show it.

"Next I shall best you at eating garlic-soaked mushrooms!"

"I look forward to the challenge, sir," said Bapa Jim, as cordial as you please. "The process of losing promises to be delicious!"

"What say you to a spot of fencing?"

"Fine!"

"And then a competition where we make pencil drawings of each other's faces!"

"I'm game, sir."

"With our eyes closed!"

"All right."

"Marbles?"

"If I can pick my own dobber."

"It's called a goom."

"Begging the president's pardon, sir, but I think you'll find if it's not a dobber it's a tronk."

"Never! I say if it's not a goom it's a bumboozer, a noogie, or a taw!"

"Not a cosher?"

"Hardly!"

"As you wish."

"There! I've won at naming the plumper!"

"There's simply no getting the better of you today."

"I should say not! Not today, nor tomorrow, nor any day at all!"

"*Vive la France!*"

"*Vive la France!*"

Five hours later over a game of straight pool, with the president in the lead by a comfortable sixty-two balls, the conversation finally turned to the reason for Bapa Jim's visit.

"I wonder," said Bapa Jim, "what's your latest thinking about the troubles in Morocco?"

"Troubles?"

"Your massacred countrymen, your excellency."

"Pish posh, as the English say."

"Do they?"

"I don't know."

"You're not concerned?"

"About what the English say?"

"About the massacred Frenchmen."

"Would it be churlish to point out that there are no massacred Frenchmen?"

"It's just that it's in all the papers."

"That doesn't make it any truer."

"Not to you or me. But what about world opinion?"

"I see, I see, world opinion, yes, world opinion. Well, what of it?"

"Perhaps nothing. The do-nothing option is certainly on the table for you if you don't mind living with the impression that the French will stand by and do nothing about a putative massacre of its apparent people. I can imagine Bertie's face!"

"Never!"

"Never!"

"Three in the corner."

"Tricky."

The president missed the three but the nine went in the side.

"*Merde,*" said the president.

"Did you not say the nine?"

"Did I?"

"I'd love to say you didn't but unfortunately I'm sure you did."

"Very well then. Yes. Yes, I'm sure I meant to in any case. I'll just carry on. And this Moroccan business, do you know what, the world can expect a manly response from the French people, I can tell you that much indeed. Truths, falsehoods, reality, delusion. It matters little. Trifle with the French at your own peril, that's what I say!"

"So," said Bapa Jim. "An occupying force?"

"*Oui,* of course!"

"Sizable?"

"I daresay."

"A sound plan, your excellency. I couldn't have advised you better myself."

"The Combined Principalities aren't going to like it, naturally."

"I imagine the Moroccans won't be wild about it either, but what can one do?"

"What one must!"

# Chapter Twenty-Four

"What one must!"

The president sighed.

"Is it a proportional response though?" he wondered aloud.

"Would you like my advice?" asked Bapa Jim.

"I wouldn't trust anybody more."

"Announce that it's just a temporary state of affairs intended only to calm the situation down. Everyone will admire your restraint and you will have seized the moral high ground. Once you're there, of course, anything goes and stay as long as you like."

"Hurrah!"

"Hurrah!"

# Chapter Twenty-Five

"I've got a girlfriend now," said Saho, causing silence.

It wasn't true. Saho did not have a girlfriend now. Saho had wistful bad feelings about when he used to have girlfriends.

"Well, that's great," said Bapa Jim when the silence was used up.

"A girlfriend," said Matalulu with a playful push on Saho's shoulder.

"When do we meet her?" said Bahena.

Ding dong said the doorbell.

"That'll be the Chinese," said Bapa Jim.

"All of them?" said Bahena, causing her father to point at her approvingly on his way to the door.

The delivery man from their favorite Chinese restaurant was there, the hole in the wall, the one where the twins worked and did synchronized head turning and smiling at you when you went there in person, hypnotizing you into thinking of it as your favorite Chinese restaurant. The man handed over the plastic bag containing the paper bag containing the boxes containing the food in exchange for money, and as he walked away, he revealed in Saho's imagination a pale, skinny young woman with stringy black hair who had been standing just behind him. Bapa Jim would look at her quizzically if she were really there.

"I'm invited," she said in a thinly defiant voice in Saho's head.

I would tell everyone that I invited her over for dinner, thought Saho, and they'd all be surprised. She'd come in and look at everyone suspiciously. Everyone would know she must have liked me too because she showed up. She'd look around and say something.

"What is this?" she'd probably say. "You live with these people?"

They'd be polite to her. They'd hasten to invite her to sit down, to have some Chinese. She'd be wary, defensive, attractive. She'd be challenging. Not offensive but on the offensive. The conversation would be awkward. There would be hardly any of it. They'd be curious about her but they wouldn't want to sound nosy. They'd ask the normal questions and it would disgust her with how boring such questions were. How disappointing.

"Gimme some of them dumplings," she'd say abruptly. They'd give her some.

To the external observer, Saho was just sitting there distractedly with an unsettling half grin and his lips moving strangely. Bahena tried not to think about doors flying open and being grabbed and dragged down into the darkest shadowy recesses of basements by jackies. Matalulu had a faraway look and she was humming quietly. Only Bapa Jim seemed present, but he was so present that only the food mattered; he attacked it eagerly. He steadfastly ignored the feeling that things were amiss, that nobody was there with him. All was quiet. All was quiet here.

There was so much nobody knew, thought Bahena. She could drop a bomb about her clients. What would her mother say? What would her father? When she was a little girl, he would stroke her hair and answer her questions about which he'd rather be, a dog with a cubical head or a butterfly with laser eyes. Things had changed. He'd probably pick cubical head now. Maybe not. Who knows?

"Well, let's see," said Bahena, reaching for a fortune cookie and pausing to crack it open.

She pulled out the little piece of white paper with red writing. Occasionally, one gets a doubler: two fortunes in the same cookie. In this case, Bahena had pulled out three: a tripler!

Time slowed to a crawl. Matalulu had just begun a head shake to get her hair over her shoulder; her hair now moved in barely perceptible motion, her eyes in glacial mid-blink. Saho a study in sadness. Bapa Jim lost in the sweet and the sour, unaware of events around the table, unaware even that he was stuck in time.

Bahena read the first fortune. It said: Speak forthrightly and be rewarded. Hmmm.

She read the second: Secrets will eat you from the inside out. The third: Do it now!

There were also numbers on each slip. Bahena would play them in Powerball but she wouldn't win.

Time became normal again. There was no tripler. Bahena hadn't even reached for a fortune cookie yet. Nothing had happened. No time had passed. Bahena felt mischievous.

"What would you rather have," she asked the table. "Wheels instead of legs or fingers like spaghetti?"

"Could I have spaghetti wheels?" asked Bapa Jim.

"No," said Bahena.

"Dang it," said Bapa Jim. "I don't know. Spaghetti fingers."

"Why?" asked Bahena.

By way of suggesting the answer, Matalulu wiggled her fingers all around, let her hands flop around her wrists.

"Exactly," said Bapa Jim. "Thank you."

Matalulu continued wiggling her fingers at him a little bit too long, smiling a little too strangely. Everyone ignored it.

"Although maybe I'd have wheels," said Bapa Jim. "Zip around."

"Spaghetti fingers," said Matalulu.

"Could I use your bathroom?" That's what Saho's girlfriend would say at some point if she were there. She'd receive permission, of course, but only after the slightest horrified delay. What would she do in there? Everyone would worry. People like that might do anything in a bathroom alone. Anything from overdosing to dipping their toothbrushes down her underpants. The time she was gone would be torturous. While she was gone, with the sound of her chair scraping the floor still hanging in the air, nobody would speak for a thousand years.

I bet my clients could vaporize everyone, thought Bahena. They could make everyone hang in the air until I said they could come down.

My girl would tell stories that nobody would know how to respond to, thought Saho. She'd just blurt them out. She'd say she got punched in the stomach yesterday. Everyone would be silent.

"Hey!" said Bapa Jim, as if waking from a trance. "I've got a story for you. A man came upon a group of five hundred thousand Galicians roaming through the woods crying."

"Why Galicians?" said Bahena.

"I don't know," said Bapa Jim. "I heard it as Galicians. I don't think it matters. You prefer a different group?"

"No, it's fine."

"I can change it."

"No, no."

"There are lots of woods to roam through in Galicia."

"Go with it."

"A man was in the woods when he came upon a group of five hundred thousand Galicians. They were crying. He asked them why they were crying. They told him, we're lost, and we're all alone."

Everyone smiled, especially in Saho's mind his girlfriend, only everyone was sorry that they'd seen her teeth. Matalulu, thinking that life was hard, thinking serenely of her own troubles, smiled again, especially at Saho, and tried to make it a loving smile, not a sad one. Saho saw both aspects, but it made no difference since he immediately told himself he'd seen nothing. By the time he went to sleep that night Saho had forgotten all about his girlfriend but in his old age if he made it that far he'd be convinced it had all really happened. This one girl, he'd probably say, oh, and he'd start laughing, she was mad as balloons, she came over for dinner one time, well you should have seen my family, they hardly knew what to say.

# Chapter Twenty-Six

What do other people do when they find themselves deeply in debt to the mob? What do normal people do? Matalulu considered her options. Number one: pay them back. This was implausible. Where would she get the money to do that? She liked the romantic ideal of robbing a bank and driving away in a convertible, firing guns into the air and trailing scarves. Not only that, but she believed herself to be such a sympathetic figure that no jury, hearing the context, would convict her, and if they did, no judge would give her a very terrible sentence. However, in the end she rejected the idea. She gave herself a few reasons, but they all boiled down to not having what it takes to rob banks.

She could go and try to murder everyone in the mob but no.

Change of identity? Plastic surgery?

Fleeing.

She had always considered fleeing to be a noble art, one which may appear superficially to derive from cowardice, but which actually requires enormous courage. To flee was to throw caution to the wind, to break one's chains, to forswear obligations, to make a classic leap of faith, faith in naught but leaping itself. Without crushing debts and violent gangsters, Matalulu might never have discovered within herself what it takes to bust loose.

"So, it's gotten that bad, has it?" said Bapa Jim.

"I'm afraid so," said Matalulu.

"Is she even well enough to travel?"

"Just," said Matalulu. "I think it'll do her a world of good to take the waters."

"Don't we have waters here?"

"Not like in Finland."

"I see," said Bapa Jim, and then after a pause: "Are you sure?"

"You don't want me to go. I won't go."

"No, no, of course you must go. If that's the best thing for Aunt Gina, that's all I need to know. I'm just curious is all. Finland. Obviously, they invented the sauna."

"The Finnish baths are legendary. They are Aunt Gina's only hope."

"Well, it's settled then. Just be sure you appreciate that they're Nordic, not Scandinavian, that's my advice. I'll give you some jokes about the Swedes. The Finns do have a sense of humor, especially about the Swedes, it's just that they're very comfortable with silence and they mean what they say."

"Thank you."

"Shall I go with you? It's high time I met Aunt Gina and if there's anything I can do, anything at all..."

"You're a saint, but no, of course, it's not necessary. This is all very womanly."

"Of course. Well. If there's anything I can do."

"Of course."

Matalulu's choice of Finland was based on a combination of factors. It fit the criteria of being unlikely to occur to gangsters as somewhere to look for someone, of being substantially but not drastically remote, and of having a magical aspect of what the Finns call *vakava ja hauska samalla kertaa*. To say nothing of the famous saunas. Also, she had no intention of going there. She had no idea where she would go. But having said it out loud at random, she thought why not. Matalulu went to Finland after all.

She knew she couldn't stay away forever. She had a family, among other things. This would be a limited-term flee. A chance to reflect in Nordic safety without having to look over her shoulder. She just wanted to buy herself some time. Perhaps a solution would occur to her. Perhaps the Finns would have an idea. Perhaps she would experience what the Finns call *epätavallista luovuutta*.

There was nothing about the journey that felt real and at no point did it seem like she was really going to Finland. At no point did it seem like Finland was really a place, certainly not really a place one could go. She landed in a place they'd have you believe was really called Helsinki and wandered into the airport, which seemed anything but real. It was an airport from the future, all shiny curves and cleanliness, with a small central garden of rocks and trees that looked like it was a careful preservation of all that remained of planet earth in the year 4001. She was invited by a female android to name the airport after herself temporarily, but Matalulu felt that putting her name in neon lights above the airport's front entrance would not be conducive to the secrecy she was after. This was not real, surely not real, very much unreal. Too cinematic. High concept. Antiseptic bleak meets wry deadpan. Matalulu resolved to leave so-called Helsinki. She wanted to see what else there was.

The Finnish urban airport simulacrum had realistic rental cars, so she got one. It started, just like a real car. The car moved when she put it in gear, just like a real car. They drove on the same side of the street she was used to, but there wasn't enough traffic. They clearly hadn't been able to hire enough fake drivers. She was being nitpicky. It must've all been pulled together for her on short notice. She herself had only decided on Finland so recently; it's amazing what they'd accomplished in practically no time. Matalulu lit a cigarette and smoked it in defiance of presumed Finnish law while driving away from the city, slowly at first and then faster, drawn by lakes and villages, certain she would look back on all this one day and believe she had dreamt it. She might be dreaming it right now.

Trees. Lakes. Villages. She drove for something between forty minutes and three million hours and stopped the car to breathe the northern airs and stretch her legs. When she first emerged from the car, she was shocked by how cold it was. She looked at the sky. It had stars, just like the real sky, only more of them, and just a little bit o'er bright. She looked around. It was a village. There was a frozen lake. She left the car where it was and walked.

There was a nice public park, and a little further along, another one. Between them, public gardens, with a few incongruous wildflowers defying the temperature. Matalulu sniffed the air and smelled rich heritage, antiquated crafts, artisans' wares. Nobody was ice skating. Was she the only one here? No. Just over the road, next to a well-preserved factory museum, a bustling café. Matalulu went in straight away.

She imagined that as soon as the door shut behind her everyone would stop talking and eating and there would be silence and they would all stare at her, but to her surprise nobody paid any attention. *They're good, these Finns*, she thought; *real good*. She found an empty seat at a booth and sat in it. Between one and a thousand minutes later a waitress came by and said:

"*Mitä saisi olla?*"

"I'm so sorry," said Matalulu. "I haven't even thought about the language."

"It's all right," said the waitress, whose name was Pihla. "Seventy percent of Finns including me are fluent in English."

"Why is Finland different from Sweden?" asked Matalulu.

"Oh, well..."

"Because the Swedes have nice neighbors."

Pihla trembled silently in a way that indicated she thought Matalulu's joke was hilarious, and her finger curled in the Finnish equivalent of slapping the table hard four times.

"How do you know a Finnish man is madly in love with his wife?" asked Pihla.

"He, he, uhhh, he... how?"

"He almost tells her."

"Ha!" laughed Matalulu out loud, causing everyone to stop talking and eating and create silence while they stared at her, but only for a span of time between nothing and hardly a moment.

After a meal of cabbage rolls and squeaky cheese with cloudberry jam, Matalulu was faced at last with the void. Neither eating nor fleeing, but having eaten and fled, the sense of pointlessness threatened to become overwhelming within Matalulu's breast and cause unfathomable despair or what the Finns call *käsittämätön epätoivo*. What was she doing here? Where was she going? To what, to whom was she connected? Was she mad?

Pihla, like all Finns, knew the void and recognized its symptoms. Sizing up Matalulu's expression from her position by the coffee machine, she reckoned that this foreign woman was in the throes of *hiipuva riemu*: the first flush of the post-euphoric stage of fleeing when the heart is most vulnerable to black existential dread. Like all Finns, Pihla knew what to do about it. Her shift was over anyway. She took her apron off, hung it on a peg, and walked in a purposeful yet unassuming manner to Matalulu's booth.

"Come," said Pihla. "*Bastu.*"

Pihla took Matalulu out of the café and around a corner, through an alley, out onto another street, and ultimately to a *puulämmitteinen kylpylä*: a wood-fired bathhouse.

"Sauna," said Matalulu, and Pihla just nodded.

It was all very wooden and clean and smelled of cedar and steam. They were welcomed by two female sauna shamans with their heads wrapped in special towels and smocks on their bodies. The shamans spoke of the *löyly*, the sacred steam that bridged the mundane and the divine by creating a liminal space between the living and the dead. As they entered the sauna, they spoke of the sauna spirits. They rubbed Matalulu and Pihla all over with organic peat and encouraged them to breathe with a sense of presence. Then they handed Matalulu and Pihla some birch twigs.

At first Matalulu thought she was meant to smell the twigs, probably with a sense of presence, so she started sniffing serenely. The patience of the shamans' smiles and Pihla's hand on her shoulder indicated that she had gotten the wrong idea.

"Like this," said Pihla, gently flagellating herself with the twigs.

"Ah," said Matalulu. She began to flagellate herself gently as well, awkwardly at first but earnestly seeking some sort of rhythm or technique to make an art of it. Slap slap, flappy flappy slap slap.

As the new friends flagellated, the sauna shamans made chants and whistles to the spirits of the steam. After that, Matalulu and Pihla were given small glasses of Sima, a sparkling mead made from raisins and lemons. The fine line between cloying and delicious.

The sauna shamans cleared their throats, nodding significantly.

"All right," said Pihla, turning to Matalulu. "Up."

Matalulu and Pihla stood up and as they stepped out of the sauna, they were given slippers and extremely thick fluffy robes, robes that could be given a season-five rating if they were sleeping bags, warm enough to make Matalulu wonder why a robe needed to be so hardy. Her question was soon answered, as the sauna shamans led the two of them out of the nice warm bathhouse entirely and into the frigid night air. It was a short walk to the pier by the lake. Matalulu grew concerned. Why did the shamans have a saw?

A: To cut a circular hole in the ice on the lake.

Did Matalulu jump or was she pushed? It is very difficult to say. Pushing can take so many forms. Matalulu was suddenly in the ice-cold lake, submerged, shocked, full-body brain freeze, exhilarated. She came up gasping to see Pihla and two sauna shamans laughing not at her, but with the omni-connection and into the steam.

"Come out!" shouted Pihla, extending a hand from the pier. "It's my turn."

It was only later over a drink at a surrealist Finnish burlesque club that the conversation turned fortuitously to cabaret.

"Cabaret?" said Matalulu. "Here?"

"Yes, of course," said Pihla. "It's very popular."

A connection with a theme; the beginning of meaning. Matalulu's feeling of *turhanpäiväisyys* began to transform into a sense of destiny. She asked questions. She learned that Finnish cabaret was elaborate. It's not just singing with a touch of dancing and the occasional juggler.

"No," laughed Pihla. "It's everything. Carnival. Satire. The most popular forms are those that savage the bourgeoisie most ruthlessly. And do you know who the most eager customers are?"

"The bourgeoisie."

"They pay good money for it."

Matalulu felt cleansed by the various Finnish treatments she had encountered. She had sent her weakness into the sacred steam to be carried away by the sauna spirits and she had fortified her *henki* in the icy waters. She had sistered with the burlesque. She was ready serenely to face herself with devil's eyes and return to the land of her troubles. Gangsters? Debt? Gangsters Schmangsters. Debt Schmedt. She would bring some Finnish back with her. She would bring it to The Broken Goose. When she arrived back home, she was just in time for dinner.

Bapa Jim asked her how it was and she said fine. He asked how Aunt Gina was and Matalulu was momentarily thrown off her game, but she recovered enough to report that Gina was sickly. She was a sickly woman, but the trip had done her good.

# Chapter Twenty-Seven

In fact, the sickliest women in northern Europe *was* in Finland at that time – the same time Matalulu was there. Moreover, her name was Gina, and she had a nephew, although he avoided her because she was so sickly. The point is: she was an aunt. She was one of an unknown number of Aunt Ginas. Was she an aunt to anyone else? Could she have been in some sense materteral to our Matalulu? Was it just possible that, despite Matalulu's deceptions, life had done one of its things where the lie you told was truer than you thought? Could the irony be that Aunt Gina was precisely where Matalulu said she would be, at the precise time, unbeknownst to Matalulu herself?

We must sometimes take an apparently preposterous idea very seriously if we don't want to fall victim to our own narrow assumptions or, if you will, our programming. There is no shortage of cases where yesterday's preposterous idea becomes today's obvious reality and we are left astounded at the limitless stupidity of the human mind. Let us sort it out and weigh it up.

Sickly Gina was, in a word, bungled. She was a bungled animal who had long since stopped tracing her origins to any conception of the divine. She had listened to too many people. She had lost any sense of her own instincts. She was no longer a poet of her own life, neither in small matters nor in large. She admired those who wielded character with style and assumed that she too would somehow rise to that same height. She did not, or rather, had not yet, and had no conception of the way. While this state of affairs resulted in her considerable suffering, it also made her interesting. She was interesting in that her torment was self-inflicted, a result of a bad conscience, not from any bad deeds, but from the oppressive regularity of her overly civilized and routinized existence. What mortified her the most was her realization that, despite the wildness of what she still believed to be her essential nature, despite what she'd like to believe, she had become calculable.

Gina had a crippling fear of the law and of punishment. It's not as if she had criminal instincts. She had committed no legal transgressions, engaged in no corruption, was in breach of no regulations. Far from it. Yet she felt the overweening power of the state most keenly and walked as if hunched over, as if the sky were a low ceiling dotted with surveillance drones, walked apologetically, on eggshells.

She'd always been this way. As a child she'd had infantile paralysis and pneumonia and polio and scarlet fever and found that her brain felt always on fire and her left leg began to twist inward. But whereas Wilma Rudolph, from similar yet even more challenging circumstances, overcame her polio and her leg braces to become the fastest woman in the world, an Olympic champion and, as if that weren't more than enough already, a civil rights and women's rights pioneer, Gina instead became overwhelmed by the sheer indifference of unapologetic matter-of-fact nature.

She knew enough to understand her failings. She knew pain. She knew that the great needed and embraced pain and faced it and went through it and used it to become greater, whereas the ordinary tried merely to avoid pain. Gina could neither avoid nor embrace hers. She lived with her struggles, and the effort was visible. Detectable effort is what robs character of style. This, too, Gina knew and could do nothing about. The path left to her was the way of wandering in an attempt, or one could say a hope, of somehow stumbling into a state of overcoming her melancholic dispute with herself and serenely inhabiting a constantly renewing reverence for being.

That's why she went to Finland. What angry gangsters were to Matalulu, estrangement was to Gina. What she did not want was for life to take pity on her. What she wrestled with was her dependency on her own anguish. Would the famous saunas help? Would the tradition of flagellating with twigs? Would jumping into ice-cold water? Would asking a taxi driver to play music in the car without paying royalties to the artists in flagrant violation of Finnish intellectual property law?

Perhaps. It is difficult to say.

Could this, at last, be our own Aunt Gina, a woman drawn by unseen forces toward a convergence with a Matalulu whose own mental processes had woven an invisible yet powerful bond between them?

However much we might wish it to be so, clinical genealogists have determined to an accuracy of 99.437 percent that it is what they charitably call highly unlikely to be the case. The most intractable optimists among us will seize on the difference between unlikely and impossible and cling to that 0.563 percent chance that this is the miracle for which we have all been hoping against hope to find. To them, we in our lab coats among our beakers and instruments with our skeptical and irony-tinged squints raise our crystal glasses in a hearty toast. May their enemies live long enough to see them vindicated. May the improbable not be irreproducible. May peace be upon the winds of eternal mystery. *Hölkyn kölkyn!*

# Chapter Twenty-Eight

Bahena went out on a date with a man for the first time in a while. How did it happen? She often ate lunch alone at a café near where she worked; so did he. They had seen each other a few times. Fleeting eye contact with quick look-away. Unbeknownst to Bahena, the fellow had developed a small crush on her. One day, all nervous, he had dared to approach her table. He bent over, squinted at his own hand, and made a tiny opening and closing mouth with his fingers. Without quite looking directly at Bahena, he spoke to her.

"What am I doing?" he had asked.

"What?"

"What am I doing? With my hands."

"No idea."

"Come on!"

"Seriously," said Bahena. "No clue."

The man stopped what he was doing and looked directly at her for the first time, wearing an exasperated expression on his face.

"Making small talk!"

"That's... funny."

"Thank God. You're a regular right? How's the reuben today?"

"Oh, it's..."

"Because the huevos rancheros was a little off."

"Was it? The reuben is fine."

"Oh, good. So was the huevos. It was fine really. I like this place. I'm not a complainer."

There followed a suggestion about eating together some time and an agreement that it could happen.

Was it even a date? Her clients had taught her how to see the way things would go with a person, but she had to stick her finger deep into his ear in order to do it. She was reluctant to do that for the two obvious reasons, namely, it would transgress a number of eminently defensible social norms and it was disgusting.

It was tempting, however, because she did not wish to waste time on a futile and painful dead end. This fellow had a boring first name that spoke of football games and damp aspirations and she was not wildly attracted to him to begin with. Bahena also did not feel herself to be wildly attractive, on the other hand. There could be no denying that she felt the tingling vibrations of fear that she was every bit as boring as he was despite her constant inner revolt against that possibility and that, furthermore, life was ultimately a boundlessly disheartening exercise in pointless resource consumption for which an early voluntary exit was the least unbearable solution. Yet her clients were undeniably fascinating, certain scientific questions remained intriguing, trips to the beach were nice, she was in the middle of not one but two dramatic series on streaming services to which she was absolutely addicted, and she had seen some of her older friends and colleagues hold out unrealistically for dream men until they were suddenly lonely in their mid-fifties with infinitesimal prospects.

For her part, Bahena considered herself a realist; she would give this middling man and life itself a chance. Perhaps he would prove to be tolerable, even occasionally amusing, maybe tender. Perhaps life-affirming surprises instead of the kind that suggested a genetic propensity toward madness could still occur. She would have an open mind.

They went not to dinner but to their usual lunch: a boring choice of date, if that's what it was, yet also a standard if ambiguous beginning and difficult to fault except for an excess of caution. The café itself? The same place they both always went anyway. The only thing that changed was that they agreed to sit together. To order together, eat together. Bahena began the affair in strained-patience mode. She sensed that mister boring name had the same reservations she did and was playing it safe; she would do the same.

She limited herself initially to anodyne comments about unremarkable topics, slowly introducing abstractions, testing out minor witticisms, eliciting blank looks, hoping to hear something that couldn't have been mindlessly absorbed wholesale from a professional view-shaping outlet, something that intelligently reflected a consciousness of the absurd, the insane, the complicit, the unknown.

"I'm a Christian," he said at one point unpromisingly, "but honestly? I'm sorry but we need to do more to protect our borders. The situation is absolutely..."

"If I told you who I worked with you'd probably call the FBI, the NSA, NASA, and Homeland Security even though none of them would do anything to me. Say something stupid."

The face of the man with the boring first name turned into a mashed potato landscape into which someone had pressed a wire caricature of bemusement.

"Wow," he said. "Frankly that's all a bit too..."

Bahena practically leapt across the table and stuck her finger as deeply as she could into the surprised man's ear. She wiggled it in and furrowed her brow in the manner in which she had been taught by her clients. After a brief struggle in which the fellow kicked his little feet around and failed to re-establish sovereignty over his own head, she received a clear vision in a series of neuronal impulses. It was a vision of a boring man now in his fifties with uncontrolled alcoholism and increasingly severe rosacea who would eventually hit her hard in the face once before ultimately being eaten alive by ants made of his own self-loathing.

"No thanks," she said, removing her finger from his ear and wiping it on her tights. She walked out of the café without another word, leaving the man to look back some time soon and tell the story of the date, if that's what it was, to his friends, if that's what they were, in an understandably uncomprehending and patently inaccurate way. Bahena would need a new place to eat lunch.

She went back to work feeling, perhaps counterintuitively, exhilarated. She had, after all, successfully avoided making even the slightest compromise for the sake of a potential relationship, the looming inadequacy of which was readily apparent even before the neuronal visions, never mind the long-term prospects, which had been categorically revealed as disastrous. What could have been decades of unrewarding effort in a doomed cause had instead been dispensed with before the arrival of the mediocre appetizers.

Therefore when she went into the communications room back at the office to meet with the clients it was with a smile on her face.

"You were so right," she said to the one who had taught her, kissing his tiny hand. "I owe you one. Big time."

The client made noises equivalent to laughter and I told you so. Bahena told him the full story through a series of forehead wrinkles, and they shared a bit of banter by way of mystery vapors. The client had had some hilarious relationship failures in his day as well. Soon the pitch of the conversation subsided enough that Bahena's underlying troubles were noticeable to both of them. After a little prodding, she admitted that she was plagued by a sense of randomness and a feeling of trying not to admit that everyone in her family was secretly very strange.

"I sometimes feel like I just need to get away from it all," said Bahena.

The client made a noise like a squamous marble-stuffed pork belly being chewed on by a Patterdale terrier, which Bahena understood to mean, in a very significant and suggestive way, that getting away from it all was well within the spectrum of possibilities.

She arched an eyebrow curiously and invited the client to continue. Who wouldn't be interested in a little trip on a super futuristic spaceship to see the sights?

# Chapter Twenty-Nine

The deepest human-made hole on earth? That would be the Kola Superdeep Borehole at 12,262 meters true vertical depth, over seven and a half miles down and only nine inches in diameter. Kola Superdeep. The borehole to end all boreholes.

"*You're* a super deep borehole," said Sonny.

"It's a Russian hole near the Norwegian border," Saho explained. "Deepest man-made hole on earth. But you couldn't hide in it. You couldn't sink down into it and disappear. Tie a long rope onto something and lower yourself in? Nope. No can do. It's only nine inches wide. You couldn't fit. Average shoulder width is what – sixteen, eighteen inches? Two feet? Maybe one of those weird bone people who can fold themselves in half. Probably not even. I doubt you could even stuff a baby down there. But Christ, I wish I hadn't even said that or thought it, who would even try that, hopefully nobody. Somebody would. Somebody out there would try it."

"You could fit if you had no bones at all," said Sonny.

"I suppose so," said Saho before continuing. "If you had no bones and you greased yourself up real good you could get in there and slide for miles. You would just keep going and going for longer than you could even believe. Now, it's not the *longest* man-made hole. It used to be. The Al Shaheen oil well in Qatar is the longest now, but it goes sideways for a while. It doesn't go as deep."

"Who's Al Shaheen?"

"Don't be an idiot."

They were sitting on top of a dumpster behind a convenience store drinking vodka out of bottles that were still in their paper bags. Sonny took a long gulp of his so Saho took a small sip and compared himself favorably.

"I'm serious," he continued from his superior position. "It used to be Bertha Rogers in Oklahoma. She's not a person, don't make a stupid joke. It's a hole, the Bertha Rogers hole. A little less than ten thousand meters. It was a depth record for a while. Respect. But Kola Superdeep blows it away now. But Al and Bertha, they were oil holes. Kola was a science hole. They just wanted to see how deep they could go. They wanted to go as deep as possible."

Sonny made a joke about Saho being as deep as possible, and Saho said durr hurr hurr and told Sonny to shut up. There's no way he was as bad as Sonny. He was a genius compared to Sonny. Sonny gulped again and Saho sipped. Sipped twice.

"You probably expected they'd run into the basaltic layer at about seven kilometers down," Saho said. "Right? That was the theory, but it was all based on seismic waves, interpreting seismic activity. They didn't have any samples or anything. They looked at the waves and they were like, there's a discontinuity down there at seven kilometers. They were like, you'd have granite, and then it would be basalts. Basalt, that's volcanic rock, OK? Fine grained. Low viscosity. Totally extrusive. Keep that in mind. It's extrusive. Nothing like granite. That would explain the waves, the discontinuity. So everyone's like, fine."

"Keep going," said Sonny. "This shit is fascinating."

"Right?"

Saho kept going.

"I love holes," he said. "Deeper the better. Anyway, they get down to seven kilometers and there's no basalt. What is there?"

"Fire?"

"Fire. Please. No. More granite. But it's granite that went through a metamorphosis. That was the discontinuity. The metamorphosis."

"What kind of metamorphosis?"

"You know, metamorphosis. Change. The kind where the rock changes."

"Yeah, but what did it change into and why was it still granite then? Did it change or didn't it? Like you're saying it's changed but it's still granite? Bullshit."

"I don't know," said Saho. "Shut up. Don't worry about it. You take that on as a project. You go find out. It's granite but it's granite with a difference. That's all you need to know. The point is the change itself is the discontinuity. It's deep granite. Probably more dense. Seven kilometers of earth on top of it, it's probably compressed. Dense."

"You're dense," said Sonny.

"Oh my God," said Saho. "Anyway, also, there's not supposed to be water down there but there was. It shouldn't be there, that was the theory, but nobody told the water so there it was. And hydrogen. They pulled out mud that was absolutely literally boiling with hydrogen. Totally unexpected. And all of that so far is nothing. They also found life down there. Changed our understanding of life. It wasn't supposed to be there. Extreme pressures, extreme temperatures. Not hospitable. Not conventionally. But guess what. Microscopic plankton fossils. You heard me. You see what I mean? You go deep, you learn things. Learning is change. Change for the better. This is why I like holes. It's a metaphor about metamorphosis. It's *metaphormosis*."

"OK," said Sonny, chugging the last of his vodka bottle and hurling it into the bushes behind him even though he was sitting right on a dumpster.

"And now it's abandoned," said Saho, looking wistfully at the back end of the convenience store. "You wouldn't even know it was there if you stood right over it. You'd look down and see a tiny old rusty-looking hole cap nine inches wide covered in trash and dirt and crap. I've seen pictures. Here. I'll show you."

Saho found a picture of the abandoned Kola Superdeep location on his phone and showed it to Sonny, confirming his description of the state of the project today. Sonny looked at it and couldn't remember what it was a picture of or why Saho was showing it to him.

"Looks like crap," he said, figuring that was true no matter what.

"Yep," said Saho.

Sonny informed Saho that he had to roll. He made the small leap off of the dumpster to the surface of the parking lot, landed ungracefully, fell awkwardly on his side, and got up as if nothing had happened.

"Later," he said.

"Later," said Saho.

Sonny staggered off and was soon lost in shadows. Saho sat there for a while longer, sipping, his mind going into holes. He eventually slid off the dumpster and landed on his feet, but he did not go straight home. Instead, he went into the convenience store. He had enough money for a pack of cigarettes but not enough for a pack of cigarettes and a bag of potato chips.

The situation called for a bit of shoplifting so Saho began to emanate suspicious vibrations, looking around too much, hunching his shoulders, standing at unnatural angles. He picked up two bags of potato chips and tucked one under his arm inside his jacket. He continued to look at the other one, pretending to read the ingredients, pretending to be unhappy with them, putting the bag down ostentatiously. He knew he shouldn't whistle, and he didn't whistle, but he couldn't stop his lips from pursing into a half-puckered whistly shape. Fortunately for Saho, the clerk was paying no attention to him whatsoever, even when he paid for his cigarettes awkwardly with one hand while pinning an eighty-decibel crinkly bag of potato chips to his rib cage with his other arm. Saho made a silent benediction to clerkish apathy.

Then he traversed the parking lot, crossed a few roads, and began to walk across the big dog-walking field, the one by the mental hospital, the one where sometimes you could see ostensibly crazy people sitting on the grassy slope. Some had committed crimes, some were former children, sometimes they were with attendants, sometimes not, sometimes glaring or smiling, seeming gone. Saho walked across there, almost as if he were nosing around for trouble, searching for small rusty hole caps, going Kola Superdeep.

# Chapter Thirty

"Excellent idea to have our meeting out of doors, sir!" said Anna, the Kaiser's advisor on public health. "So good for the heart and lungs!"

Madeleine and Karl nodded their agreement. The Kaiser looked down from his perch on the frame of an affordable house he was helping to build in a previously disadvantaged community.

"Glad you approve, Anna," said the Kaiser. "Are there enough snacks?"

"Plenty, sir!" said Karl, the Kaiser's advisor on industrial affairs.

The Kaiser had decided one day that meetings didn't have to be boring. They could be more like parties. There could be food. And why not beer and wine? There was no reason work couldn't be fun, within reason, of course. One could even enjoy the vigorous pleasures of construction work while holding perfectly productive discussions.

"You're doing a lovely job on the houses, sir," said Anna.

"Thank you, Anna!"

"And you're setting an exemplary model of what it means to be a true leader, if I may say," added Madeleine.

"Just doing my bit, Maddy, just doing my bit."

"Well, you're certainly putting equity and justice at the forefront of your efforts, sir!" put in Karl.

The Kaiser permitted himself a smile, only to feel ashamed at the rush of pride he felt surge in his veins.

"It's not about me, my friends. If we're going to combat systemic injustice, we're all going to have to do our part. It is the courage of others that humbles and inspires me to put my own shoulder to the wheel of decency here today."

Madeleine got busy doing a bit of edgework in preparation for planting some hollyhocks that had been assembled in pots along the pathways.

"Should we, erm, grab a hammer and climb up to help?" offered Karl hesitantly, not at all sure he wouldn't make a hash of it if he tried.

"Only if you'd enjoy the work," said the Kaiser, "but I wouldn't advise it if you've also been enjoying the lager!"

He winked at Anna, who was at that moment pulling herself a pint from the keg.

"One a day," she said, only slightly defensively. "It's actually very good for you."

"So good you sometimes have two!" teased the Kaiser.

"Even three!" said Anna, to peals of good-natured laughter.

"Does nobody like blue cheese?" asked the Kaiser, lining up the next roofing nail and making sure his grip on the hammer was light yet firm. "It's wonderful with the bruschetta. I hate to see those squash blossoms just sitting there, that's pimento ricotta you know."

"I hate to bring up business," began Karl.

"Not at all," said the Kaiser, expertly banging in the nail that would do its part to keep one family warm and dry. "Quite right. Don't mind me, I'm multitasking but I'm listening keenly I assure you. Update me. Are the people happy and healthy? Are we committing enough resources to clean energy, bike paths, preventive and therapeutic health care, marginalized communities? Are there enough buckwheat cheddar blinis with smoked salmon for the population as a whole, bearing in mind the fourteen percent who prefer it without smoked salmon?"

Anna spoke frankly and invited open discussion about the status of their goals for a thriving civil society. She concluded that they had done quite a lot, and that things were pretty good, that they had exceeded their targets, but if they were to ask themselves honestly was the job done? No. There was more yet to do. This was not the time for complacency and pats on the back. The people could be even happier. They could be even healthier.

"And industrially?" asked the Kaiser. "Are we on track for demonstrating to the world the benefits of our clean and efficient state-of-the-art technologies so that all might reap the rewards of our revolutionary production processes?"

"We are," said Karl. "At the rate we're going, we'll be able to meet not only the basic needs of the people but plenty of their wants as well, and with a fraction of the work required."

"Does that mean..." began the Kaiser.

"Yes. We're on track within five years to see a Combined Principalities where folks won't have to work more than three hours a day, and perhaps four days a week, in order to have comfortable, sustainable lives."

"We're anticipating an enormous boom in the arts and sciences," said Madeleine, the advisor on arts, sciences, and gardening. "And gardening."

"What fantastic news," said the Kaiser, silently scolding himself for glancing covetously at some pancetta-wrapped peaches with basil and aged balsamic while there was still work to be done. "What a splendid state of affairs. What a beautiful world. What an awe-inspiring universe. You see what we can do with a little bit of good will, some hard work, and hearts full of love? I can hardly wait to tell Uncle Bertie and let him share the fruits of our discoveries with his people."

For a few moments the grounds fell silent with the reverberations of full hearts, but for the sound of discreet chewing of some corn and chanterelle crostini and the stirring stridency of some mistle thrushes singing in the middle distance.

"Excuse me! Sir!"

It was Gunther who had run up, the Kaiser's advisor on foreign affairs, late to the meeting and all out of breath. The

Kaiser placed his hammer down gently and gave Gunther his full attention. Gunther was an earnest fellow and a hard worker and rarely appeared unless there was some sort of emergency. He kept a weather eye on events outside the Principalities and nobody knew better than he which ones could be ignored and which ones bore reporting upon.

"Ahoy there, Gunther! Have some blini!"

"Sir! It's..."

"Hang on! No sense shouting it all up at me. You're too excited. Let me come down."

The Kaiser climbed down the scaffolding, dusted himself off, and clapped old Gunther on the shoulders.

"Do continue," he implored.

"It's the French, sir," said Gunther.

"Ah, the French," chuckled the Kaiser good-naturedly. "Those French. Couldn't you just kiss them, the little roustabouts! I'd like to tousle their hair! Oh, what kind of mess have they gotten themselves into this time?"

"It's Morocco again, sir."

"Of course it is!"

"Well, you remember how some months back the French sent a sizable contingent of troops to Morocco in alleged response to some sort of apparent massacre despite it being against the Recognition of Interests of the Combined Principalities Act? Specifically, the Paragraph on Non-Intervention?"

"Technically speaking," said the Kaiser, with a detectable note of reproval in his voice.

"Yes, technically," said Gunther, with a matching note of apology. "I don't mean to be a fastidious little stickler; I just thought it bore mentioning."

"Oh, indeed!" said the Kaiser, cheering up. "Someone's got to attend to the details. Forgive me."

"Not at all," said Gunther. "It's just that, you know how they said it would be a small presence for a short time?"

"Yes, for their French pride, that's why we looked discreetly the other way and didn't make a fuss."

"Exactly. Well, it turns out it's a large presence and it's not going anywhere."

"Hmm. A large long-term presence now, is it?"

"I'm afraid so, sir."

"They're incorrigible is what they are."

"It's an affront, sir, to put it bluntly."

"Just as you say. We'll be expected to have some sort of response."

"I hardly think we can just sit back and do nothing."

The Kaiser sighed.

"Yes, I suppose so, but it's hardly worth putting lives at risk over. Oh, send a small ship with a few guns to look a bit stern off the coast, will you? That should shame them into looking at themselves in the mirror. A small one, now, Gunther. I hate guns and we don't want to look like maniacs."

"Just the one?"

"Certainly. I think they'll get the message. They've made their point, we'll make ours, honor is served, everyone goes home happy, and I can get back to the important work of improving real people's lives in the communities where they live!"

Everyone looked up at the structure under construction and admired how it was coming along. They shrugged at the fairness of what the Kaiser had proposed.

"That's going to be a nice house," said Gunther.

"It certainly is," replied the Kaiser.

So it was that a lone small gunboat was sent by the Combined Principalities to the coast of Morocco in a show of official irritation.

# Chapter Thirty-One

Bapa Jim met with the Greeks. He met with the Portuguese. He met with the Belgians, the Russians, the Italians, the Danish, the Japanese, the Romanians. Everyone had to be told about the Kaiser's outrageous preparations for war with his massive fleet of enormous gunships on the way. Finally, he called in on his old friend, his majesty Bertie the king, who was sitting in a hot tub surrounded by youthful roister-doisters.

"Jimmy!" cried Bertie, slapping his porky hands on the water excitedly. "Come in! Get in here!"

"Dear God, no," said Bapa Jim, smiling broadly. "Hot tubs do terrible things to my skin. I break out in tiny volcanoes, it's awful."

"Like so much of what we do, a classic example of something that only appears to be terrible but is actually beneficial in the longer term. It's part of the cleansing process, my friend. Clears you right out."

"Well, I'd better do it some other time in private then. I couldn't bear my volcanic drippings polluting the communal tub water. I'd be mortified."

"Bah," said Bertie. "I daresay they wouldn't be the most dreadful drippings in this water!"

"You certainly make it sound enticing," said Bapa Jim, "but I think I'll stick to my guns in this instance and keep my powder and everything else dry."

"Suit yourself! What news do you bring me?"

"It's getting hot in Morocco, Bertie."

"It's always hot in Morocco, Jimmy!"

Bapa Jim laughed, eliciting a confused frown for a moment from Bertie, who then decided he must have made a joke and had better join in the laughter.

"Tell me everything," continued Bertie, "but first let's get some food. The only thing worse than exciting news is exciting news on an empty stomach."

Bertie paused here but decided he had not made a joke and that the lack of laughter was therefore appropriate. He ordered his companions to disperse, climbed out of the tub, dripping everywhere, and shook his entire heft vigorously like an outsized terrier coming out of the surf. His wibblies wibbled; his jibblies jibbled; his wang dang doodled. He snapped his fingers and a subservient brought him a merciful towel. Bapa Jim opened his eyes.

By the time they had been whisked away, stopped for a couple of quick public appearances for the popular Bertie's adoring crowds, and were finally ensconced in a royal dining chamber, a distinct air of melancholia wafted around Bertie's countenance. Bapa Jim politely pretended not to notice until it became clear that Bertie was going to be ostentatiously melancholy until he was conspicuously noticed. Bapa Jim sighed kindly.

"What is it, Bertie?"

There followed a few oh nothings and oh come on nows.

"Well," said Bertie, "if you must know, it's Mummy."

"I see."

"I'll tell you everything. Someone's threatening to name me as a co-respondent in a divorce suit, very annoying, a trifling matter really but you know how Mummy is when these things hit the rumor mills."

"She... doesn't always understand the demands of your lifestyle."

"Exactly! Well put!"

"Who is the divorcing party, if I may ask?"

"Ugh. Let's just say he's a member of parliament and likes nothing better than to take potshots at me while professing loyalty to the crown and adoration for my mother."

"Disgusting."

"I think so."

"Oh for the days of beheading, am I right?"

"You said a mouthful."

"Surely he could be paid off or blackmailed."

"Oh, probably but it's not just that."

"I'm loath to be nosy…"

"Bless you. But you already know about my taste for actresses, dancers, singers, nobility, wealthy humanitarians, prostitutes, and the like."

"Certainly. In short, women."

"Well, I'm not entirely indiscriminate."

"Most women."

"That's fair. And the odd fellow. And Mummy never liked it."

"No."

"But since my marriage she's been positively insufferable about it."

"Has she got some sway over you? Can she cause you trouble?"

"Politically? No."

"Then…"

"Am I not human, man? If you prick me and so forth? Emotionally, Jimmy! Emotionally!"

"I'm listening."

"She says… dear God."

"You needn't say it."

"I must."

"All right."

"She says the sight of me makes her shudder. *Shudder!*"

Bapa Jim nodded and allowed a silence.

"That's rough," said Bapa Jim at last. "Even for a king."

"It's not just the philandering either. She detests everything about me. She thinks I'm a shallow unthinking buffoon, unworthy of the crown. Callous. Selfish. Stupid. I make her ill. She experiences physical revulsion. My own mother."

"She thinks being shallow, unthinking, and a buffoon makes a person unworthy of the crown? This much, at least, is refutable."

"Goodness knows I've tried to be discreet. A king has appetites, naturally, an earl, a duke, a prince, a knight of the realm, yes, appetites, a lust for life, a sense of daring, a taste for fun and adventure, a king, a man, alive, strong, full of heart, a living roar, is that so wrong? Is there no deference? No discretion? No decency?"

"It is in short supply."

"I am a wretch. Mummy is right."

"Nonsense."

"You're right, of course. I've done more for the crown than anyone in generations, made public appearances, been popular, appeared human."

"You single-handedly made Norfolk jackets fashionable."

"I pioneered the pressing of trouser legs from side to side."

"You've supported the arts like few before you."

"I practically invented Sunday dinner. I've built European alliances, played baccarat, promoted the unity of class-free human feeling through music."

"You entertain on a lavish scale."

"Yet I'm a lowdown dog of a man, a scoundrel, a faithless scalawag."

"You? The man who instructed the British foreign service to treat people in India with the same dignity as anyone else? The man who introduced the stand-up turn-down shirt collar? Never! I'll not have it!"

Bertie got out of his chair and walked around the table. He wrapped his enormous arms around Bapa Jim, lifted him into the air, squeezed him tightly, and pressed his wide face into Bapa Jim's belly. Tears flowed freely from royal ducts.

"You understand," said Bertie. "You perhaps alone in all the world."

"Of course," said Bapa Jim, but the strain in his voice made it clear that he was having some difficulty breathing. Bertie set him down and returned to his seat.

"Now then," said Bertie. "Enough about me. Weren't you going to tell me something about Morocco?"

"Indeed I was," said Bapa Jim. "It's not good news, I'm afraid."

Bapa Jim reported to Bertie that the king's own nephew, the top man of the Combined Principalities, had taken aggressive, threatening, warlike steps. The Kaiser had sent an enormous fleet of gunships, extra-large ones, to Morocco to threaten the French. It could only mean that the Kaiser desired war and was making preparations. The king should check with the allies. They were all alarmed. A robust response was demanded by the angels of history.

Bertie had never really liked his nephew. His mother was wild about the guy.

# Chapter Thirty-Two

Saho wandered across the dog field by the mental hospital and tried not to think too much about why the patients were in there or what it must be like inside their heads or how different or similar it might be. Well, Saho reckoned, who was he to judge?

During the day the field was full of dogs running around chasing each other or just going in mad circles like they were trying to catch ghosts of themselves who lived half a second into the future. But at this time of day, well into the night, there were no dogs, except perhaps the ghosts still swirling. Saho had his little vodka bottle, he had his cigarettes and his bag of potato chips, he even had half a joint tucked into his coat pocket that he had forgotten about.

At night the dog field seemed darker than it ought to be, like if it had a basement it'd have jackies in it. Not only were there no lights, but the field itself and its ring of trees seemed to repel any ambient light from the surrounding area. You could still bring a dog, but most people didn't. There would be no point in throwing a stick for fetching. If you threw it for any distance, you'd have no idea where it ended up and neither would the dog. Nobody else was on the field but by instinct Saho kept to the darkest, most shadowy bits by the trees at the edge, near where the mental patients, or lunatics as Saho affectionately called them, would sometimes be allowed out to smoke cigarettes. He slid along the grass like an oil spill, justified in feeling like a person would need special glasses to see him, glasses that would also allow them to see disappointments and jokes that people didn't get. He bumped along to the music in his head.

One moment Saho was there on the field slinking and bumping along and the next moment he wasn't. He had fallen into a hole.

The hole – Saho was guessing – was about fifteen feet deep and about five feet wide. Not much of a hole for mankind but quite a drop for a man. It might have been a well, but Saho was still guessing. There wasn't any water at the bottom and there weren't any buckets. It was dry, and soft enough so that Saho was more surprised than injured. Surprised and indignant. The whole thing made him feel like he was ten years old, except there should be one of his pals up top looking down at him, apologizing for having pushed him into the well. Or there should be a faithful dog, a real one, a real dog that was his and that would run to the nearest tavern and bark in such a way that people would eventually understand that they needed to follow him back to the well.

Someone would have to be blamed for this, leaving open holes in the middle of fields in the cold dark night where anyone could drop into them. There would be a lawsuit. Saho would be rich. This was his lucky day. Finally, he'd have some money of his own, some real money, which would transform his life. He paused briefly to appreciate the blessing of having been born into a litigious culture.

Saho made a cavalier attempt at climbing up out of the hole. It consisted of looking upwards, poking the side of the hole with his finger, and giving up. He would have shouted for help but how embarrassing. All he could do was picture what that would be like to somebody who wasn't in the hole. A voice from the ground screaming help. It would be terrifying or hilarious. What it wouldn't be was dignified. Saho only felt that he deserved dignity when he was at his most ridiculous. So, no shouting or screaming. If he heard anyone walk by, he might call out casually, as if saying good morning to a passing neighbor while bringing in the milk delivery. Otherwise, he would simply wait for the light of the new day when the holemaker would no doubt return to continue the work on his dubious ill-conceived project.

There would certainly be dogs in the morning, other people's real dogs, and one of them was bound to put a snout in and start barking. Some dog owner's face would appear above peering down obtusely, trying to comprehend what it was looking at. Saho would have his arms folded, would make an ironic face, maybe even hurl an insult. Are you going to stand there all day with that stupid look on your face or are you going to throw me down a rope? If you think I look like a moron, you should see yourself. Take a look in the mirror. Jackass. Squinter. Gaper.

Saho tried to lean against the wall there at the bottom of the hole but he fell down right on his own bottom like a slapstick clown. There they were, hole and man, two bottoms, together at last. The reason he fell down is that there was no wall at that part of the hole to lean against: there was another hole, a sideways hole. A tunnel.

He did briefly think about rats and weasels and foxes and earthworms and wire worms and millipedes but despite all these horrors, to say nothing of the unknowns, he went in. It was not a tall tunnel. He had to walk all hunched over, like a monster.

# Chapter Thirty-Three

At the next family dinner nobody noticed that Saho wasn't there because in his place was a phantom Saho, ever so slightly translucent but otherwise a perfect mimicry of the real deal. Bapa Jim was dealing out the food so Phantom Saho didn't have to move a muscle, he just sat there and looked somewhere between his plate and the rest of the world, in precise mimicry of Real Saho. Like surveillance in Foucault's panopticon, the place of Saho need not be occupied, its potential must simply be believed in.

Light is always changing and creating new shadows, so that even perfectly still objects like Phantom Saho can appear to be animated. It's not as if Real Saho was much of a conversationalist these days anyway. It had been years – decades – since he'd excitedly brought up stories about what he'd been up to or people he'd met or funny things that had happened, or since he'd shown anyone pictures he had drawn or said anything about a cool bike he wanted to have. It used to be a lively regular thing when he was a boy. He used to be the life of the party, bright as a button and twinkles in his young eyes. There's no sense mourning this kind of change. "It has come," as the Ugandan scientist said in placid resignation about the invasive water hyacinth. "It is with us."

Matalulu smiled like her mind was somewhere else entirely and the people around her at the table represented the minuscule comings and goings of book lice.

Helping herself to some peas, Bahena nearly noticed that Saho seemed distant somehow, nearly thought that there were probably some families that had big conversations and possible touches of hysteria when one of them seemed to have gone phantom. She did have rather interesting things going on in her own life and worries enough to boot. People can be forgiven.

"So," she said, because she was feeling crazy enough to try to elicit a question about what she had been up to personally, "anything interesting happen to anyone lately?"

"I rode a bus," said Bapa Jim cheerfully. "Fantastic. Super efficient. Perfectly pleasant. You should have seen the driver. Said hello to everyone. Brightened everyone's day."

A bus, thought Bahena. That's nice. Rather earthly though. Not quite as interesting as the things that happen to me. I do like a nice bus driver though.

"And how was Finland?" asked Bahena. "How's Aunt Gina?"

Matalulu looked at her and smiled the smile one smiles at a hamster in a wheel.

"OK then," said Bahena, smiling at her mother the way one smiles when one has clients from extreme places that nobody would believe.

"Hey," said Bapa Jim. "Did you know you can actually hear the blood in your own veins?"

"Wait," said Bahena. "What?"

"Sure," continued Bapa Jim. "You just have to listen varicosely."

It hit Bahena's funny bone; she shot fizzy water through her nose.

"Hey," said Bapa Jim. "Remind me. You lost your job a while back, right, or am I crazy?"

"Um," said Bahena, "well, there was a job at one point a while back that I did lose, yes."

"Well don't worry," said Bapa Jim. "You'll find something."

"Thanks," said Bahena. "And what about your job? How's the advertising game?"

Bapa Jim made a facial expression that was hard to interpret, something between eh not too bad and eh who knows and eh shut up.

"Super," he then said.

They ate for a while, not in silence because there were lots of sounds: silverware on plates, scraping, the sound of chewing, the strange bony sound that Matalulu's jaw made when she chewed that was not a normal chewing sound and that made Bahena want to scream. And there were ambient sounds: a car door slamming somewhere, the washing machine, things that only dogs could hear. Goodness knows what spiders are listening to.

"Saho," said Bahena after this period of non-silent not-talking, "you should eat, what's the matter?"

Now there was true silence because the entire universe went on pause and time itself stopped and noise became a null possibility. It might have gone on for only a moment, it might have been imaginary, and it might have stayed that way for millennia. Nobody would have aged. There would be no way to tell. But it must have started up again at some point because history continued.

Like any impostor, Phantom Saho was concerned that he'd have to act like Real Saho now, only he lacked the ability to eat or talk or laugh. He concentrated as hard as he could on manifesting a facial expression, any facial expression, and the light caught him in such a way that people could see whatever they wanted in his face.

"He's not hungry," said Matalulu, thinking of what Saho had been like as a cute and intelligent little boy but not smiling because she was too busy gripping tightly onto the handrail of her own life.

"Not a problem," said Bapa Jim. "Make you a snack later, OK, kid?"

Phantom Saho panicked and desperately tried to look real, and Bapa Jim saw a smile.

Bahena, Matalulu, and Bapa Jim, each of them shrugged either physically or mentally, or both. It has come. It is with us. One Saho being a little translucent isn't headline news these days.

# Chapter Thirty-Four

When Matalulu next entered The Broken Goose, she knew Big Tony would show up sooner or later. Probably sooner. She was ready to face him and the mob with Finnish fortitude. She didn't know what she would say or do. She only knew she would maintain a serene sense of *mielenmaltti*. Upon crossing the room, she found Louis sitting in a pose of afternoon dejection, head in hands, moaning. Next to him sat Madame Dandelion, maintaining a stony face except to roll her eyes for the benefit of Matalulu.

"Trouble in paradise, baby," said Madame Dandelion. "He's been like this all day."

Matalulu slapped him hard in the face.

"Ow!" said Louis.

"I thought it might snap you out of it."

"Where you been?"

"Finland."

"Of course," said Louis. "Why wouldn't you be?"

"What's the matter with you?"

"I owe two months' back rent on this place, I'm pulling in doodly squat, and now my cheek stings."

"You can get big loans from the mob," said Matalulu.

"Thanks for the tip," said Louis.

"Face it," said Madame Dandelion. "This place is dead."

Matalulu looked around. The place did not look like the cabaret of her dreams. It had not yet been Finlandized.

"What about these guys?" she said, nodding toward the back of the club where a mixed group of poets and magicians sat around in a huddle.

"Them?" said Louis. "They don't have any money."

Matalulu stood up and walked over to the group. They knew who she was and several stood up to bow theatrically before her, but also pointed at one of the magicians as if to say, watch this, we're in the middle of something. The magician was bending a spoon with her mind and the others were cracking jokes but watching carefully. She held the spoon lightly with just two fingers on the handle and stroked its curved neck with one finger of her other hand. The spoon began to bend. She lightly moved her finger around the bowl of the spoon and the whole length of the handle began to twist. When she was done, the handle had twisted five or six times and was bent over at least sixty degrees. She handed the spoon to one of the poets, who pushed and pulled on it to see if it was an easy-bending trick spoon.

The poet shrugged and handed the spoon to Matalulu, who inspected it carefully and gently tried to bend it, the normal way, with her muscles, just as the poet had done. The spoon would not budge.

"You're a tricky one," she said.

They laughed. One of them stood and pulled up a chair for Matalulu and insisted that she sit down with them. She did, and proceeded to explain and suggest things, gesturing and eliciting more laughter, eliciting claps.

From his table on the other side of the floor, Louis became curious. He lifted his head off of his hands and peeked in Matalulu's direction. She was speaking in low tones that Louis couldn't make out, but she was emphatic about it. She pointed forcefully, now at a poet, now at a magician, now opening her hands as if revealing a new planet. The group of them appeared to be mesmerized. When she finally finished speaking, she slammed her hand down on the table, pushed herself back in her chair, and folded her arms. They stood. Matalulu was kissed, had her hands taken, was bowed to.

*What on earth*, thought Louis.

Matalulu glided back over to the table where Louis sat stewing in curiosity, skepticism, hope, fear, dejection.

"What?" said Louis. "What, what, what, what, what?"

Matalulu explained that the group, and not only that group but their friends and artistic acquaintances, were going to liven up the joint.

"Oh yeah?" said Louis. "Do I get a say in it?"

Madame Dandelion and Matalulu looked at him.

"Of course," said Matalulu.

"Might as well see what they've got," said Louis, looking down.

"Them and their friends," corrected Matalulu.

They set about it that very afternoon, starting with decorations. Implements of torture and murder were arranged throughout, along with smiling child's doll heads, protest placards, items of lingerie, judges' wigs, feather boas, parasols, and plague-doctor masks.

The outside was festooned with brightly colored graffiti portraits of kings who abdicated for love and artists who quit to paddle canoes in hot countries. A street bench was placed directly next to the front door, and on it a lyric poet performed his interpretation of a man dying friendless and alone.

An actor with the stage name Nether Again engaged in chilling theatrical portrayals of man's instinctual drives. His one-man play Awakenings, written before lunchtime, was banned before its first performance after the police were tipped off about how shocking it would be to the bourgeoisie. The news only stimulated the public's outrage about the goings-on at The Broken Goose.

By late afternoon, four poets who had dubbed themselves the Executioners stood wearing blood-red gowns, their heads covered by cowls with the tiniest slits for their eyes. Charlie the piano player slammed dissonant low notes with the edge of his fist as the group muttered monotone threats in an insistent rhythm and shook their axes at the audience, except for one who stood corpse rigid and emitted an unnerving stare.

A bohemian gentleman stood up and declared that City A lives, while City B merely functions, while behind him a live donkey painted a large canvas with its tail. When he finished his pronouncement, the gentleman congratulated the donkey and, before leading it off the stage, introduced a girl who could stare at you until you cried.

A group of secessionist painters set up shop in one corner of the club and, wearing unflattering swimwear, furiously churned out acrylic works symbolizing the group's contempt for pleasure, surrounded by carefully curated objects stolen from the local prison.

A garment worker read aloud from Bakhtin next to an elderly woman who worked marionettes into rude poses. They were joined by a German shouter of imprecations, damning onlookers for being full while he himself had to go hungry. *Spürt meine Leere, ihr wohlgenährten Mastschweine!*

The Heeby Jeeby Baby, nearly seven feet tall, roamed ceaselessly around the neighborhood handing out flyers and insulting people in broken French in the name of The Broken Goose. *Au nom de L'Oie Rompue, je remarque ton embonpoint!*

Two artists who were in love with each but never dared to confess it immediately set to work producing a house magazine in arch style, including poems, artwork, cultural commentary, impossible puzzles and contests, and feature articles on selected performers.

The evening proper opened with an uncompromising shadow play followed by poetry, composed entirely on the spot out of random text selections from beauty magazines, on the theme of urban "variety nerves."

Next, a severe-looking woman took the stage in flaming colors and performed a socio-critical dance pantomime that elicited approving cries of "pornography!" The spotlight on her was intentionally harsh. Next to her sat a bored-looking man on a stool reading a newspaper. The woman began to tense herself up, her fists tightening into white-knuckle balls, her shoulders all hunched, her buttocks and thighs clenched so tightly that the distortion of her face by pain was nothing if not real. Her skin seemed to whiten to the point that even bearing witness to it made one feel the numbness.

The man on the bench looked up from his newspaper and said: "She is alive."

Then very slowly she began to relax, one body part at a time. Her face softened but did not become any more beautiful. Her fingers uncurled. Her legs stretched and bent and her shoulders dropped. If she'd gone any more limp, she'd have fallen like a rag doll, but she remained standing, only suddenly her head fell, stopping at an alarming angle, like a broken doll.

The man looked up from his paper again, frowned at the woman, and said: "She is dead."

They both stood up straight, held hands, and bowed to the crowd, which received them warmly.

The last act before Matalulu was a small fellow called Palu with darting eyes who spoke quietly from a wooden stool about a man he wanted to murder. He had good reasons and a clever plan, and the victim had no family himself and would be mourned by nobody. Palu could reasonably expect to get away with the crime.

"Still," concluded Palu in almost a whisper, "what I don't know is whether, having done it, I'll be able to bear it."

He received warm applause and a few shouts of encouragement, not limited to the local mafiosi. He continued to sit thoughtfully until Matalulu herself took the stage, whispered in his ear, put her arm around his shoulders, stood him up, and walked the first few steps with him until he had momentum.

"Thank you all so much for coming," said Matalulu, feeling the electricity of the collective anticipation. The lights went down, a hush descended, a frisson of vital energy skizzled through the room, and at the precise moment that people absolutely could not stand it anymore, she looked up dramatically. The spotlight hit her, she closed her eyes, and she sang.

Even Big Tony, having entered quietly, standing discreetly at the back of the room, was moved. He took his hand off of his piece and clapped as hard as anyone when she was finished. But then he put his hand back on his piece. That's where he liked his hand to be. In his pocket. Right on the old piece.

He made his way to Matalulu, who saw him approaching, and he was, if he was honest, slightly unnerved by her steady eye contact.

"You did good," he said when he arrived at her side, still fingering his piece. "But we gotta talk. Tomorrow night. Show up."

# Chapter Thirty-Five

One theory about Aunt Gina that gained early currency held that she was the subject of a certain painting by a notorious Romanian artist who was given to wearing green uniforms with gold embroidery and epaulettes and indulging in scandalous affairs with the wives of prominent politicians. The extent to which this particular putative Gina was herself entangled with said artist is neither here nor there; it is enough that the portrait remains as a tantalizing if inconclusive clue as to her true identity.

Presuming for the sake of argument that Aunt Gina was a really existing person and that this was her portrait, we can draw a few tentative conclusions. First, this Gina is known to have been born in a castle in Ireland, proving at least that the rumors that her mother was not pregnant, which circulated widely at that time, were false. The precise date of her birth is the subject of some controversy, with baptismal certificates, newspaper reports, and county filings all at odds with one another insofar as date, month, and even year are concerned. Gina herself was evidently entirely uninterested in resolving the matter to anyone's satisfaction, saying only that she was content to receive gifts and congratulations on any date of anyone's choosing.

As for the castle, the Gina under consideration has frequently said that it wasn't a real castle, because it was never intended for defense, but only for entertainment. It had a large ballroom, a drawing room, a lesser and a greater dining room, at least one morning room (which Gina pointedly insisted on enjoying in the afternoon), a library, and a showpiece hall with ornamental corbels and world-class stained glass windows. Its essentially frivolous character notwithstanding, it had every appearance of a real castle: it sat on the highest point of a vast expanse of land, it was made of stone, and it had towers, crenellations, bretèches, and turrets, lacking only drawbridge and moat. However, Gina's conviction that the castle lacked reality played a profound and formative role in the development of her sense that delusion was at the core of every society – that people, all of them, everywhere, were mad.

When Gina was three, her father was appointed to a diplomatic post in Mumbai, so the family moved to India, where that same father promptly died of cholera. Her mother, who was still only nineteen, remarried within the year to an army lieutenant called Delaval, who regarded young Gina as being spoiled and half-wild. He called her a "queer, wayward Indian girl" and, after she spent an entire church service sticking flowers into the wig of the elderly man sat in the pew in front of her, Delaval – with no record of opposition from her mother – had Gina sent back to the West and enrolled in a boarding school. There she developed a reputation for having a fierce determination and an even fiercer temper, until she was sent to another boarding school, and then another, until at age sixteen she eloped with her own army lieutenant. Gina and her new husband went back to India, where she soon divorced him for having cholera and dying within weeks of their arrival.

It is at this time that Gina makes her first truly radical, if not entirely uncharacteristic, break with the normative social fabric of her upbringing. She takes the stage name Lola and becomes a professional, that is to say lurid, dancer. While attracting notoriety in this capacity, she made the mistake of embarking on this new career without first fleeing to a new location. Therefore, stage name notwithstanding, she was widely recognized as the lieutenant's wife, generating some of the scandal that draws the world's and indeed our own attention to her in the first place. When it became clear that the net effect of all the kerfuffle on her life, spirit, and finances was negative, she picked up and moved to Copenhagen, which is in Denmark, a country that is as Nordic as it is Scandinavian.

In Copenhagen Gina, as Lola, began to accept favors from a few wealthy men, to the extent that her profession was generally regarded as courtesan, although she continued dancing. She even made a legitimate stage debut dancing in a minor opera by a lesser French composer, an experience she was to describe as "personally disappointing" for reasons she declined to specify.

As disenchanting as the opera may have been for her, the experience nonetheless served to introduce her to the inner circles of the city's literary Bohemia. She became the mistress of some of the best-known composers of the day, both classical and popular, and an intimate of several of the greatest women novelists in Europe. One of her conquests was a fellow we shall call Alexandre, who was the owner as well as the drama critic of the newspaper with the highest circulation in Denmark.

Alexandre's association with Gina can be said to have led directly to his premature death at the hands of a valorous banneret. Unhappy with the attention Gina was receiving at a lavish party of the cultural elite, a drunken Alexandre quarreled with her bitterly and loudly, knocking over an ice sculpture and half the buffet table in the process. He managed to offend the chivalrous horseman to whom we have just alluded, who came to Gina's aid in a show of concern. The two men subsequently engaged in the duel that honor demanded, and in which Alexandre was run clean through with a saber. The headline still ran on the front page, but the drama section was thin for weeks afterwards.

Gina was to leave Copenhagen for Brussels, where in public the Belgian king conspicuously demanded to know whether her breasts were real. Without a word she is said to have torn off garments one by one until the question was definitively answered in the affirmative. The king was as enamored as the crowd were shocked, and her influence on the royal prerogatives was subsequently as great as her unpopularity among the ordinary people, whom she regularly treated to outbursts of anger and contempt. Despite vocal opposition from mobs on the royal front lawn, the king made Gina the Countess of Flanders, a title that came with a sizable annuity.

As the power behind the throne, Gina ensured that every official who opposed her entitlement was demoted to humiliating positions. She made it illegal to criticize a countess, punishable by fines of up to two weeks' wages or a month in prison. Upon brief reflection she also wielded her influence to promote the cause of liberalism and to attack organized religions.

Within a few months, the king was forced to abdicate as a result of a student-led revolution, and Gina fled the country for Finland, where she married a new army lieutenant with a recent inheritance. Sadly, the young man drowned shortly thereafter, ending what had swiftly become a tempestuous relationship. It was at this point that Gina embarked for the United States in an attempt to gain distance from her past and to rehabilitate her tarnished image.

In San Francisco she married a newspaperman who, while not a drama critic, was very critical of the theater in private conversation. This marriage, too, soon failed, and a co-respondent in the divorce proceedings brought against her – a cardiologist named Tim – was murdered shortly thereafter, poisoned by a dart flung from behind a rustling curtain. Although rumors and suspicions abounded, the case has remained unsolved.

The rehabilitation of her image had not gone well, and she arguably did it no favors with her sensational performances of her one-woman play, Lola!, in which she performed an erotic Crab Dance involving lifting her skirts high enough to establish that she was not wearing anything underneath. The play was called "utterly subversive, even by San Francisco standards" and, as a result, respectable people were forced to stop patronizing the theater that had hosted the show, crippling the venue, whose heavy losses soon forced it to shut down entirely. Daunted but not defeated, Gina took her show on the road and performed it *in situ*, Crab Dance and all, at coal mines to enthusiastic audiences of diggers. During a journey on a steamboat to stage a performance at a construction site in Baton Rouge, Gina's now-manager, a diminutive fellow from Hackensack called Rinky, ended up overboard and drowned in the swift current of the mighty Mississippi.

The last Gina was heard from in public life was delivering a series of lectures on morality written for her by a publicity agent and pamphleteer whose title of Reverend was of uncertain provenance.

There are rhymes here, hints, allusions, echoes that suggest that it may not be academic overreach to suspect that this, at last, is finally the Aunt Gina for whom we have been searching. Were we pressed for genetic, documentary, or anecdotal evidence linking this Gina-Lola to our Matalulu, on the other hand, would we be able to produce a single solitary tangible shred?

The answer is no.

# Chapter Thirty-Six

Bahena's repeated reference to her "clients" has attracted the attention of psychologists specializing in avoidance behaviors. In particular, her use of that term is a form of what is known in the literature as *choris circum* or, colloquially, "dancing around." To the trained clinical mind, it begins to appear that Bahena goes out of her way to avoid using the word "aliens," suggesting that she consciously or unconsciously experiences something about the latter term as a stressor.

Wilkins *et al.* suggest, perhaps counter-intuitively, that coming right out and saying "space aliens" would not make Bahena's life or her job sound more interesting, even though it would be difficult to think of a more fascinating job than working with space aliens. The problem begins with the understanding that few people would be prepared to believe such an assertion, and the subject is sophisticated enough to understand that going around saying she worked with space aliens would yield undesirable social results. She could find herself, if not openly mocked, certainly consigned in the privacy of her associates' minds to one of the categories associated with unreliability and condescending amusement. Bahena would experience their attitudinal shift via physical and emotional cues as a sense of distancing.

If something like a scientific consensus has settled around a reading of avoidance behavior, there is still lively debate over which of the several sub-types best applies: situational, cognitive, protective, somatic, substitution, or even a fluid-adaptive factor-dependent combination of all five. Academic quibbling notwithstanding, few would deny that the ostentatious use of the noncommittal word "client," specially contextualized, serves to imply aliens: half denial, half confession, putting the burden of drawing the conclusion onto the listener, as Berman and Coates deftly argue. It would, Bahena presumably hoped, be intriguing where the more direct term would simply be ludicrous. She herself by extension would be elevated to the status of a more alluring person. Lewin asserts the behavior supports a diagnosis of borderline avoidant personality disorder (although Maybury more generously demurs in favor of milder postmodern stress disorder).

The subject does not, however, successfully escape the undesirable consequences of simply calling them space aliens, owing to the transparently "stupid" (Lewin again) nature of the obvious evasion. With reference to Bahena's expression of wanting to "get away from it all" and the "clients" saying it could be arranged, we must confront the gap between wishing and expectation bearing in mind, as per William James, that the line between the material and the immaterial is notoriously difficult to draw with precision. The empiricists would simply bide their time and sharpen their pencils while waiting to see if Bahena actually gets whisked off into space at some point, literally or otherwise. Here is where the psychologists begin to yield to the astronomers.

Nobody doubts that, from a statistical perspective, the universe is very likely to be teeming with life, must be dotted with many billions of tiny blue-green planets separated yet not overwhelmed by mind-boggling expanses of pitiless barren indifference. Even so, the idea that beings from somewhere across the absurd vastness could be secretly among us on our own blue bead, no matter how tantalizing, no matter how it stimulates our most innocent wish behaviors, remains the subject of a snickering skepticism. There are the more plausible stories, not the abductions of hillbilly fabulists, not the little gray specimens that would be at home in a B-movie, but stories of air force pilots encountering impossibly fast and astonishingly maneuverable objects at high altitudes, stories that make one pause momentarily, but one retreats back to the safety of laughter soon enough, even if that laughter is perhaps ever so slightly nervous against the background of daring to dream. And once again the psychologists have their say.

In any case, even if Bahena's story were entirely true, that she worked as some sort of poorly explained liaison with aliens from outer space, it would arguably be better not to say anything at all. People would likely not be ready to hear it. It doesn't matter if a thing is true if people aren't ready to hear it. Nothing in this world, as Vondorsky put it, matters less than truth.

The sympathetic view of Bahena's awkward goings-on about "clients" is that the very ordinariness and evident decency that made her appealing as a below-radar liaison also meant she'd struggle with total dishonesty. The argument is that she simply opted for a half-baked euphemistic not-quite-lie over a full-throated straight-faced prevarication as a manifestation of Foucauldian counter-conduct.

The unsympathetic view is that Bahena just couldn't resist letting people know she had special access to guests from another world. That she knew she couldn't come out and say it, because that would be breaking the rules of the terms and conditions she had signed off on when she took the job. It would be unethical and dishonorable and possibly even illegal.

The unsympathetic view is that Bahena was desperate for external validation. The unsympathetic view is that there weren't any aliens, that Bahena had a nondescript job and a nondescript personality and that she knew it, and rather than develop skill or character she'd resort to making up outlandish falsehoods just to simulate the state of being interesting. The unsympathetic view is that she implied rather than lied simply because she lacked the courage to go all in. The unsympathetic view is that Bahena was so broken inside and so lost that she'd beg, not even for friendship, but just to be noticed, just to dream of being envied by anyone for anything for even a moment.

And that is how an unsympathetic view eventually generates a sympathetic view out of its own cruel ashes.

A sympathetic view from the empiricists is that incidentally yes as a matter of fact they did indeed take her "away from it all" and whisk her into space and give her a tour that included, among plenty of other things, a close-as-you-can-get-without-getting-sucked-in close-up of an actual black hole. What was funny was that she still had to take a bus to get home from where they dropped her off. "They" are referred to as clients because space aliens sounds inane and because that's what they were: clients. Ordinary business term.

# Chapter Thirty-Seven

Bapa Jim had organized an urgent confab of the allied elite to discuss the recent unconscionable aggression on the part of the Combined Principalities. Having stirred them up and brought them together, he reckoned it was time to hang back and let them move forward on their own momentum. While the assemblage tossed around ideas about what sorts of muscular responses were most appropriate, Bapa Jim poured himself a glass of water from the pitcher at the back of the room. Plenty of ice. He took a sip. Nice and cold.

"How much is too much?"

"How much is not enough?"

Bapa Jim smiled as the senior strategists made suggestions, adopted postures, and debated fine points. He had a sketch pad with him. People assumed, if they assumed anything, that he was taking notes. Not so. He was sketching. He had a little picture of his grandfather that he kept with him. The nice grandfather, not the mean one. It was the picture on the laminated card they gave out at his grandfather's funeral many years ago, along with the date that he first turned up on the planet and the date he skipped town, and a religious quote about valleys, evil, and fear. What moved Bapa Jim was the photograph, which was his grandfather in youthful old age, the way Bapa Jim remembered him from his own childhood.

He liked his grandfather's face and had been trying to sketch it properly for a long time. It was a face full of warmth and good humor, but also a certain reserved dignity. And he was handsome. He always looked like he might break out into some ancient folk song from the land of his ancestors, and that if he did, wherever he did it, he wouldn't really be present anymore, he'd be sitting at a fire and instead of buildings there would be trees.

It was difficult to sketch such a face. There were a lot of lines and it was easy to get them wrong. Each one was crucial. If even one was out of place or misdirected, the expression would seem false. Bapa Jim had yet to get it right. He assumed that he would never get it right but, of course, the pleasure was in the trying.

Bapa Jim remembered visiting his grandfather as a child and smelling the old-person smell of his house, even though his grandparents were scarcely sixty at the time. He would sit on the swinging bench that grandfather had on his front porch, and the two of them would sit there and watch the world go by as grandmother cooked a meal far larger than anyone cooked meals nowadays, his grandfather smoking a cigar, Bapa Jim enjoying the smell, the two of them happily untroubled by even the remotest notions of what is in retrospect the obvious sexism of the situation.

It hit him for the first time now: that must have been the old person smell. It must have been cigar smoke all up in the curtains and the furniture, mixed perhaps with sauerbraten and red cabbage. What a pleasure to put a life puzzle piece into place and finally to rest.

On the porch on the swing bench back in the day the two of them would smile and when people from the neighborhood walked by on their way to the barbershop or the butcher's or the pizzeria, they would smile back and say hello. Nobody walked past without smiling and greeting Bapa Jim's grandfather, and Bapa Jim's grandfather had a special comment for everyone. Nice hat, slim! That's the perfect color on you, Dora! Look at you, aren't you cuter than a pile of puppies! Hey slow down, Gus, you're going to take off!

Good hard worker, too, his grandfather. Worked with bricks and cement. When Bapa Jim's dad was building a patio behind their house, grandfather came over and directed the proceedings, did the digging and the raking over, built the frame out of two-by-fours, mixed the cement, poured it, smoothed it, winked occasionally at Bapa Jim, let him help, asked him for an iced tea, gave him a dollar, tousled his hair.

What a great grandfather! That's who Bapa Jim wanted to be when he got old.

Bapa Jim frowned. The times were different, the age, the circumstances, neighborhoods, the economy, the zeitgeist, the necessities. No sense in pining. It has come. It is with us.

"Jim!"

The Frenchman's cry brought him back to the room. He replied by looking up and raising an eyebrow.

"Any ideas?"

"Yes," said Bapa Jim, dissatisfied with his sketch, putting it down, wishing he was building a patio instead. "I should think some demands might be in order, unless you don't think it's a good idea."

There were nods of heads and murmurs of approval. This was a good idea. It sounded just right. Affirmations were readily forthcoming.

"Absolutely it's a good idea!"

"Demands are absolutely in order!"

"We absolutely must issue some demands."

"I for one demand some demands."

"Well," said Bapa Jim, "if you're certain."

"Certainly we're certain!"

"But, erm, well, what should we demand?"

"It doesn't matter," said Bapa Jim, "as long as it is absolutely impossible for them to comply."

# Chapter Thirty-Eight

"What is it now, Gunther?" asked the Kaiser, getting some well-earned muscle relaxation in a piping hot bath, taking a sip of the sherry he had carefully placed next to the tub on a special small table set there just for that purpose.

He regretted his impatient tone. It's just that he was just about to start reading a much-anticipated darkly absurd new novel from his favorite Latin American novelist. It had been carefully placed on the sherry table. He had taken great pains to keep it from getting wet. There had been special towels, specially placed, for the drying of his hands. He had taken care not to splash. It was going to be so lovely.

Gunther, for his part, regretted his intrusion. He knew that he was allowed to enter the bath chamber should special circumstances warrant. He also knew upon entering that he had violated a place of serenity and thought, and that he had entered it with bad news.

"My apologies, your excellency," said Gunther with a bow that spoke volumes about the sincerity and depth of his regret. "It's about Morocco. The French. They've made some demands."

The Kaiser smiled. Those French. Their pride and their stamping little feet and their demands. Couldn't you just hug them?

"Demands, is it?" said the Kaiser, his eyes all a-twinkle.

"I'm afraid so," said Gunther, his head still hanging. "And it appears they've got the backing of a considerable number of allies."

"Of course they do," said the Kaiser in his teacher voice. "Perfectly understandable. One doesn't demand things of the Combined Principalities without the security of one's friends standing beside one. It's only human. Imagine how naked and alone they'd feel otherwise. It's easy to forget how intimidating we can be with our industrial capacities and social advances but try to see it from their perspective. Why does a child make demands? When he or she feels insecure. One doesn't get angry. One addresses the root causes. One employs patience. When I was small and I had to face a conflict of any kind I'd imagine that behind me, just out of view of my peripheral vision, was an orderly streak of fierce and loyal tigers, awaiting only my command to attack. I am not trying to infantilize the French, of course. I think they're marvelous. I mean Paris, for goodness sakes. It is in many ways the capital of more than one century."

"Yes, of course," said Gunther, "but perhaps the larger or more pressing point is the demands themselves, if I may say."

"Of course you're right," said the Kaiser. "I was just getting into the proper frame of mind to hear them. To receive these demands in a state of calm reflection and loving understanding."

"That's what makes you who you are, sir."

"Indeed. Thank you. All right. Let's hear them, these demands made with the stamping of French feet and hands on Allied hips."

"They want us to decommission the entire navy and cancel all plans and contracts for building new and more modern ships."

"Done."

"Done?"

"Certainly."

"I'll be honest. I'd have thought those would've been completely unacceptable demands."

"But in fact, they're excellent ideas. What a waste of money that all is. Think what we could accomplish by diverting all those funds toward peaceful uses. The infrastructure we can build, the technological advances, the jobs we can create, the support for artistic achievements. What a relief! I only wish I'd have thought of it myself. So, although, yes, I take a certain amount of umbrage at their insolence, as leader of the Combined

Principalities my people rightly expect more of me than petulant eruptions of ego that put their lives and livelihoods on the line. I'll take their inspired suggestions. Can you imagine the looks on their faces? I can't wait to see what they come up with next!"

The two men laughed heartily and shook hands.

"I'll carry back your response then, sir."

"You do that, my good man," said the Kaiser. "As for me, I'll just add some piping hot water to my bath and continue my physical and literary immersions! I've got the children's choir later on and the Council on Underrepresented Opinions and I need to be at my cleanest and most receptive!"

# Chapter Thirty-Nine

So Big Tony wants to talk, does he? Good, because I've got a few questions for him, starting with this one: what does he want to talk about? Secondly, why? What's the point of talking? What is talking compared to doing, compared to silence?

Here's my next question: Is Big Tony even real? Is he really a mobster? Are mobsters even real? Is that what they call themselves?

Next: Who cares?

Matalulu drives her car on the expressway and smokes cigarettes. She's driving just to drive, to be in the car, to be mobile, to be alone, in control. She knows this thing could play out any number of ways.

Matalulu is seized with a sudden fierce determination. She spins the wheel of the car. The tires screech as she does a one-eighty at speed and heads for casino town where Big Tony holds court. Two hours later she slams the Hillman Avenger into a parking spot sideways, leaving rubber, gets out of the car, slams the door, flicks her latest cigarette butt into the infinite sadness hole of an unforgiving world and strides angrily toward the confrontation without looking back.

She kicks the door open. Mobsters look up. A few of them scatter at seeing the look on her face. One of them called Tearful Billy starts to cry until his pal Scabs slaps him in the face and tells him to pull his socks up.

"I want to see the big man," she says. Scabs scampers into a back room. When he comes back out, it's behind Tony and peering around the side of him. As for Tony, he stands with his hands on his hips and looks Matalulu up and down.

"Hey," he starts to say, "what's the big idea?"

But he doesn't finish. Matalulu punches him hard in the stomach. When he doubles over, she puts a knee in his face and when he groans, she shoves him backwards over a table. Tearful Billy loses it. Scabs slaps him again, grabs him by the collar, shakes him. Tony sits up. Scabs whips out his matte black gat and points it at Matalulu's face.

"Put it away," says Tony.

"You sure, boss?" says Scabs.

"I said put it away."

Scabs puts it away. Tony stands up, brushes himself off, looks at Matalulu, nods his head, smirks. He's trying to decide whether to say she's got one hell of a nerve or say that she has spunk and he'll give her that. One thing he knows is that he'll call her kid.

"You got spunk, kid," says Tony. "I'll give you that."

"We're quits," says Matalulu. "You got that?"

"Quits?" says Tony. "Just like that?"

"Yeah," says Matalulu. "Just like that."

She turns around and walks out. Big Tony takes it. He eats it. He swallows it. He's a big-hearted dumb-ass who's always had a weak spot for a kid with spunk. His mother had spunk. What the hell, he figures. It's only money. He has complexity.

Or maybe it goes down a whole different way.

Matalulu does a little sleuthing. She finds out Big Tony has a rival, an even bigger man called Louie who'd like nothing more than to see Big Tony out of the picture. She goes to see him. They find common ground. Matalulu with her access helps create a vulnerability that Louie can exploit. They hatch a plan. It goes horribly wrong and there's trouble, big trouble. In the end Matalulu is the only one left standing. She takes over the mob and makes them go legit.

On the other hand, maybe Matalulu makes her peace with her family and options are discussed. They could go with her, but after long and painful introspection, they decide it is best if they do not, at least for now. Matalulu heads back to Finland alone. She runs and she *can* hide. There are a lot of changes she has to make, but ultimately she is absorbed into Finnish society. She learns to speak some of the thirty-eight Uralic languages. She embraces relatively ascetic environmental realities and the heritage of egalitarianism, while emanating a deeply understated subtle subversive humor. She adopts a traditional livelihood and becomes emotionally connected to the countryside and nature. She develops a sense that the ice sheet that receded ten thousand years ago might one day return, and that it'll be OK. It'll be OK even if everyone dies. She develops an unconscious affinity with Kunda culture, which whispers to her from a span of seven thousand years. She feels the stone-age stare of the Kiukainen. She feels song magic and bear worship. She hums Karelian melodies. She gets the technical difference between *Joik* and *Lavlu*. She feels a kindly unconscious disdain for Swedes. She celebrates Juhannus and Vappu. She plays the throwing game *Mölkky*. She slowly eliminates silver small talk until only golden periods of silence or direct words of explicitly transactional importance remain. Conversations with baristas are limited to the kind of coffee desired and the amount of money required. It is efficient, rather than abrupt. She is comfortable with it.

When someone does ask how she is, they mean it, and she tells them, in detail. For this reason, when she makes a friend, she does it quickly. She does it deeply. There is no beating about the bush. She does not sit, walk, or stand in a way that forces her to acknowledge the presence of a stranger.

But obviously one can't count on a happy ending.

Matalulu goes on the run. She can run, but, ultimately, she can't hide. Her desperate journey ends in a dark confrontation. The bill comes due. She reaps what she has sown. She thought it was all a big laugh. Well, who's laughing now? It's the hollow laughter of the void, the most chilling laughter of all.

Maybe she never knew what hit her. Maybe it's a car bomb, a sniper shot, an ending without so much as a moment of terror, regret. No begging. Nothing abject. No humiliation piled onto her already considerable shame. One moment she's still hoping against hope for a miracle, and the next moment there's only the purity of black nothingness.

Or maybe she knows what hit her. To be precise, maybe she knows what's about to hit her. Tony steps out from the shadows. There's a glint. Something in his hand. A gun.

"End of the line, kid," he says.

"Now look, Tony," starts Matalulu, but the only answer is the flash of gunfire.

Matalulu goes down, but she has time for a few last words.

"It didn't have to be like this," she says. Or: "Tell my children I loved them."

"Yeah," says Tony, blowing the smoke off the end of his warm gat. "Sure thing, kid."

Or: "I'll say one thing for her. She had spunk."

What really happens is that Bapa Jim crosses paths with Big Tony in the nether space where intelligence agencies and mafiosi become indistinguishable at the nexus of major world political events. Jim needs to stir up trouble in the Combined Principalities in an effort to provoke a ham-fisted response from the Kaiser. Tony has the contacts to make it happen. The deal is done.

In the course of building the mutually beneficial relationship that would start hostilities, benefit strategic industry players, and generate plentiful cash, Tony and Jim allow themselves, perhaps over a manly single malt, to discuss matters that verge onto the personal. They enjoy some conversation. Their mutual association with Matalulu is not known to either of them at first, but one or the other of them eventually makes a reference to her for one reason or another.

Perhaps it's Jim, worrying aloud about his wife. Perhaps he's gotten wind of her gambling problem or has reason to suspect. It hasn't gone unnoticed that their life savings have dwindled precipitously in an unexplained fashion. Perhaps he has informants who have clued him in on her secretive cabaret career. He's not angry, just concerned for her well-being. Her mental health. He's just not sure what to do. He feels so helpless.

"Are you talking about Matalulu?" Big Tony inquires. "Matalulu, the cabaret star? Is that your wife?"

"You know Matalulu?" says a stunned Bapa Jim.

"Know her? I'm supposed to shoot her!"

They look at each other. The silence lasts for an eternity of three and a half seconds.

They burst out laughing. They laugh long. They laugh hard. They look at each other again. The laughter starts all over. They pour another shot of single malt.

They factor it into their calculations. Matalulu is off the hook. All ends well, except for the war they successfully start.

Or perhaps it's Big Tony who mentions her first. Perhaps he has misgivings about having to shoot her. Perhaps he senses Jim's qualms about his own moral calculations and wants to connect, to resonate, to sympathize. He decides to share the story about the cabaret singer that, to be honest, he not only has nothing against personally, but likes very much. Still, it's not about him and his feelings, it's about larger principles. Sometimes a man has to do what he has to do even when he doesn't want to do it. Sometimes wanting something doesn't matter. The only thing that matters is the calculation, the necessity, the required action. It may be painful, it may be dubious as hell, but the world has no time for people's feelings. It's kill or be killed, move or be moved. Tony includes a detail that piques Jim's curiosity. Maybe it's a catchphrase that Matalulu has, or some special mannerism. It makes a lightbulb turn on in Jim's head. He puts two and two together. It squares up.

"Are you talking about Matalulu?" he says.

"You know Matalulu?" says a wide-eyed Tony.

"Know her? She's my wife!"

They look at each other. The laughter thing happens. Single malt is poured. They work out a deal.

Or there never was a Tony, no debt, all figments. "It was only a dream." That possibility always comes up, we've seen this kind of thing before in countless cheap stories. It's always disappointing too so no. It was really happening.

"So. You wanted to talk? Here I am. Talk."

"I got one thing to say."

"So say it."

"The money, doll face."

"What about it?"

"Hand it over."

"Or what?"

"Or else."

"Fine."

Matalulu snapped her fingers. Would some servant suddenly appear and offer Tony a hundred and twenty thousand dollars plus interest on a purple velvet pillow with gold trim? Or did Matalulu have some goons of her own now, some fancy boys who would suddenly step out, chewing gum, slipping on some brass knuckles, twirling some nunchakus, brandishing some throwing axes?

Nothing happened.

"So?" said Tony.

"So what?"

"So the money?"

"What about it?"

Tony sighed.

"I'll give you a riddle," said Matalulu. "If you can solve it, you can have your money."

"No riddles."

"Wrong. The more you take, the more you leave behind. Name it."

"The money, kid."

"Wrong. You have two more guesses."

"You've got about two more seconds."

"One more guess."

"I'm not playing."

"Sorry."

Matalulu snapped her fingers again. Tony was gone, leaving only footsteps.

# Chapter Forty

Once most scholars abandoned the crab-dancing Lola-Gina theory as explicated previously, some turned to the belief that they had been on the right track, but that Aunt Gina was a different exotic dancer and courtesan, one who was actually called Gina, one whose eroticism was merely a cover story for her secret life as a traitorous spy known to the intelligence agencies as Agent G-21. Most people wouldn't have known either name but would certainly have heard of her stage name: Mata Gula (in Malay, literally "sugar eyes"). Here we are less concerned with whether she was an entertainer, a spy, or a scapegoat than whether she was indeed our own Aunt Gina. A review of the known facts is merely confounding.

This woman, whoever she was, was reputedly the daughter of a man who owned a hat shop and a Jewish Indonesian woman of Dutch extraction. Her early childhood has been described as "lavish" by one of her purported brothers who had investments himself in the oil industry. By the time she turned thirteen, however, hats had gone out of fashion, her father was destitute, her parents divorced, and her mother promptly died of tuberculosis and a broken parathyroid bone. Shortly thereafter her father remarried a woman from a real town called Sneek, and the now-fifteen-year-old Gina was shipped off to live with her godfather in the Moldovan city of Chisinau where she studied to be a kindergarten teacher. In many respects, this is where her troubles began.

The headmaster at her training school began to flirt with her in a manner so ostentatious as to be scandalous. You can believe whomever you like about whether she encouraged this behavior, but what's not disputed is that one day she sent him reeling over a desk during school hours with a fiercely determined punch to the midsection. So she was unhappy about something. However, she was blamed for the scandal and suffered the ensuing public outrage.

She fled Moldova and went to live with an uncle in Cochabamba, where, at the age of eighteen, she answered a newspaper ad from a Colonel Von Blatz who dabbled in ornithology and was in search of a wife. He found her agreeable and they were married according to the custom of the Cochabamba upper classes. Gina found herself in one of life's temporary reprieves, circulating freely in high society where she was able to resume the lavish lifestyle she had once taken for granted as a schoolgirl. They took a steamship to Malang where she was to bear the colonel two children.

Things took something of an ugly turn. The colonel was a heavy drinker, a poor officer, and a violent lasher-outer who irrationally blamed poor Gina for his failure to be promoted up the chain of command. He quite openly kept a concubine, which, while accepted in the Javanese culture of the time, angered his wife. Then the colonel would get angry, and he was known to bash her sometimes. Gina ultimately decided she had no recourse but to leave. She ran off with another officer in a different army and immersed herself in his local culture. Soon she'd joined a dance troupe, adopting the *nom de guerre* Mata Gula for the first time and going by it generally from that time on. Among Aunt Gina scholars the joke is that theories of her identity do not have to involve stage names and failed marriages to military men – "but it helps!"

After several months a seemingly remorseful Von Blatz promised to change his behavior and begged her to return, and against her better judgment, or in favor of her maternal instincts, she acquiesced. Unfortunately, not only were all the colonel's promises promptly broken, but both children became violently ill and died as a result of complications from treatment for the syphilis with which they had been born thanks entirely, it must be said, to the recklessly selfish Von Blatz. Unwilling or unable to kneel before the god of shame, the colonel claimed the children had instead been poisoned by an irate servant, a claim that Gina publicly supported.

Why? She had maintained the belief that, while he had been a distinctly poor husband, Von Blatz had been a good father, the drinking and the violence and the prostitutes and the syphilis and the dead children notwithstanding. It is likely that she, too, could bear neither the weight of blame nor the scandal, and it was accepted in the Javanese culture of the time to throw the odd servant under the bus in times of need. The bonds of death and deception were not enough to save the marriage, however, and after a discreet waiting period, the couple were divorced.

Rootless and disoriented, Gina – Mata Gula – moved to Paris, patching together a living as a circus horse rider and artist's model. She gravitated toward the emerging modern dance movement of that time in that place, billing herself as a Hindi Javanese princess of priestly birth and astounding audiences at the *Musée Guimet* with her fantastically provocative act, which she described as "sacred motion." Evidently nobody had seen anyone quite so carefree in style as Mata Gula, nonchalantly shedding veil after veil while making certain gyrations and maintaining hypnotic eye contact until the only thing she was wearing, other than ornaments on her arms and head, was a bejeweled breast plate. The astonishing effect of her work was not to lower her social standing but rather to elevate the art of erotic dance into respectability. She mingled on equal or superior terms with the wealthy and became the long-term mistress of a millionaire industrialist; she was the toast of Paris. The worshipful press called her majestically tragic and wonderfully strange and compared her entrancing gracefulness to that of a wild animal.

Mata Gula's heyday as a dancer endured for about five years before myriad imitators diluted her brand. She found herself emblematic of a genre now populated by dancers who relied on straightforwardly cheap exhibitionism, not bothering with the sensual or the mysterious or the enveloping mist of mythic narrative. These newcomers had otherness, but it was the wrong kind, so that the enterprise as a whole suffered reputational damage. Critics began to complain that exotic dancing lacked artistic merit after all. When one expositor from a serious cultural institution called out Mata Gula specifically for being a dancer who could not dance, her career began an unmistakable decline. She was late to the game in the first place, her bloom was beginning to fade, and the lights of the stage were unkind to the excess weight she had begun to accumulate. She ended her dancing career with a final performance that brought out a sentimental audience that treated her one last time as the star she had been, bidding her farewell with tears, love, and a standing ovation.

Her career was over, yes, but she was still Mata Gula. Still famous. Still a celebrity, if a tarnished and somewhat illicit one. She parlayed her persona into a secondary career as a courtesan for the elite – high-ranking military officers, politicians, diplomats, influential advisors. In this capacity she had frequent occasion to cross international borders, even during wartime. It occurred to more than one manipulator of world events that such a person might prove useful in the blended arts of seduction and spying. She became Agent G-21.

Long story short, love affairs were exploited, favors were requested, promises were made and broken, the wrong people were targeted, plans went sideways, important people were embarrassed, and the complex matter was resolved by throwing Mata Gula under the bus known as a firing squad. Her last act on this earth was to blow a kiss toward the gentlemen aiming at her.

But was she our Aunt Gina? There's no family tree to prove – or disprove – it. The genetic tests have not been done, and nobody is likely to foot the bill. The putative brother mentioned briefly above was located and questioned, but he denied having knowledge of anything whatsoever. Tantalizing, if you're desperate: known members of Matalulu's family, brothers of grandfathers, were indeed known to have been present at times and places where one can imagine what one likes about what might have happened.

It has also been suggested that the Mata Gula story itself was just a red herring, and that in fact it was the disgraced servant from the dead children episode who was none other than our Aunt Gina. This notion attracted keen interest from specialist researchers for a time until its originator offered only "it would be what nobody would expect" as his evidence.

So, do we have a solid reason to lay on the table right here right now? Plainly not. The good news is that the field of potential candidates can now be reduced by a minimum of two.

# Chapter Forty-One

"Sonny!" shouted Saho. "Sonny, is that you?"

Saho had only imagined it out of wishful thinking. Sonny wasn't there. It was just an empty tunnel made of dirt.

I must be missing dinner by now. I must be hungry. The thing not to do is think about the wire worms that even now cover me in a great wriggling swarm.

*No, no, my mistake,* thought Saho. I don't think I'm covered in wire worms after all. It's just me, the soil, and my rotten imagination.

"Sonny! It *is* you! What are you doing down here, man?"

"Saho?"

"Yeah, man!"

"What are you doing here?"

"What are *you* doing here?"

Sonny had all kinds of spelunking tools and things with him and he was able to produce a map, which they pored over by candlelight because Sonny had candles as well, and hadn't forgotten the matches and two or three lighters that he didn't even end up needing.

"I had no idea there were so many branches to this thing," admitted Saho.

"It's extensive," said Sonny, the uncontested superior man now in knowledge of and preparation for what was now clearly a whole system of tunnels. Saho looked at him with admiration and jealousy instead of pity.

"Say," said Saho, "you wouldn't happen to have a..."

"Sandwich? Yes."

Sonny reached into his spelunker's knapsack and produced an assortment of choices.

"Roast beef? Tuna mayo? Plain cheese?"

"Well, roast beef, please, if you don't mind."

"Not at all. Horseradish?"

"Please!"

Saho ate the sandwich while Sonny frowned at a compass and made calculations with a protractor.

"I have heard," said Sonny casually, "that in the Combined Principalities they do not fear themselves when they drink, and that this is the reason they are nothing to fear when they are drunk."

"They must not get very drunk."

"They *do* get very drunk."

"But then..."

"Then they sing."

"And then..."

"And then, when the time comes, they go home quietly."

"We should get drunk and fuck shit up in here," said Saho.

"A crude and ludicrous suggestion," observed Sonny, putting his tools back into his knapsack. "Listen. I'm going down this branch right here. I do not advise you to follow me. Goodbye. Here. Take this rubber ball. It may amuse you. Also, this flower."

Saho looked at the ball. Sonny was right: it was amusing him already. By the time he looked up all he saw was the back of Sonny marching athletically away down a tunnel branch with his spelunking tools.

Saho put the flower in his pocket, chose a different tunnel, and set about stumbling down its length. He had only just started thinking about whether there would be mole men when the first ones appeared. They were short, less than four feet tall. They had large, seemingly inflated crania. They were entirely bald on top but had hair at the temples running around the back of their heads and eyebrows so bushy it was hard not to laugh. They wore black furry woolen onesies with feet, and wooden sandals on top of the onesie feet. Their hands, too, were hairy, but beneath the hair one could see their pale and almost glowing skin. They walked as if they were half-heartedly imitating monkeys. Saho was glad to see them and he offered them the rubber ball that Sonny had given him. They took it, examined it, handed it around amongst themselves, and then threw it back. It had assumed phosphorescence. Harmless, and even more amusing now that it was glowing. They asked him if he had any oranges because that was their favorite fruit, they craved them in an almost frightening way. He said no but keep an eye out for Sonny, he probably had quite a few. Would they like a flower? He handed them his flower and they were fascinated by it. It seemed as if they were afraid of it but also trying to be brave. One of them held it very carefully and the others took turns getting their noses close or reaching out to touch it only to recoil at the last second as if they'd touched something boiling hot. Saho laughed at them and they looked at him. Then they laughed too. They knew they were being a bunch of morons.

The company was most welcome. Almost anything is endurable with a good friend by one's side, someone with whom to share the incredulity, with whom to interrogate perceptions, hold hands, make jokes, mitigate horrors. Maybe, Saho considered, if he did have a mate down in the tunnel with him, or a whole gang of mole mates, and they were in there together for a long enough time, he'd have the equal and opposite yearning for a bit of privacy. Almost anyone is unendurable given enough time in a tunnel with them. But the mole men were gone and only the glowing ball remained. They must have taken the flower with them to prove they weren't scared.

As he groped his way around a bend, Saho imagined he was at a party with the mole men and all kinds of imaginary other entities. There was his past transformed, peaceful, accepting, having taken the long view, having transcended judgment without denying accountability. Friends, acquaintances, people from previous real-life parties, people whose living rooms he had sullied, people with bathrooms that he had defiled, neighbors he had inflamed, there were the women he had treated badly, there were the furtive men, there were his embarrassments in conversation with his humiliations, there were all his angriest and stupidest moments gathered together, there were the bartenders who regretted serving him, the bouncers who had bounced him, those who had banned him, there were the stools and tables he had upturned, there were the things he had stolen, there were the restaurants he had fled without paying, all relaxed.

Saho felt free. He felt like if there was a trampoline, he'd be able to jump on it twenty feet in the air and do tricks, do them easily, do the Barani Ballout, the Kody, the Kaboom, the Arabian, the Quadriffus, the Rudy In and Out, to everyone's astonishment. If there was a skate park, he'd be able to grind and kickflip and do five-forties. This, the now, this was where it was.

Saho felt real and laughed. There will be no rehab. There will be no getting better. There will be no health. There will be no education and training. There will be no resumés. But he would get a job. It was obvious. He'd try out as one of those mole men.

# Chapter Forty-Two

Most scholars find the idea of the impossibly uber-influential suburban father figure absurd. That's not what matters. What matters to a fellow is what he'll do next. What matters to a fellow is understanding what his options are, weighing alternatives against risks, benefits, values, stakes.

Bapa Jim continues to tell little lies about big things, inventing massacres, turning token gunboats into threatening armadas, casting victims as instigators, stirring up the war fever amongst the allies, not because he's a bad person but because he thinks it's for the greater good in the medium to long term, all the while maintaining a concerned and loving presence in the home and keeping everybody smiling with the jokes at the dinner table. The global fever runs high. There's a spark. World war ensues, numerous cities are destroyed, and millions die.

Or Bapa Jim continues to tell his lies and manipulate events, but a tide of resistance begins to rise. People smell a rat. A few at first, but it's people who matter, people who can change other people's minds. Bertie's mother, doting grandmother to the Kaiser, catches wind of events and exerts her own influence. An anti-war movement is felt and gains power. An increasingly desperate Bapa Jim tells increasingly large lies, hoping that the old saying was true, that nobody thinks to disbelieve a large-enough lie, but no, for once nobody's buying. The newspapers, uncharacteristically, do journalism. They expose the truth about who's doing what to whom and the Kaiser comes out smelling like a rose. Bapa Jim on the other hand is eventually fingered as the mother of all mixers and he is splashed across the news media as a disgraced figure, a treacherous war monger, a man who puts industrial profits and great nation gamesmanship above any regard for the lives of ordinary people let alone values like honesty and fair dealing. This is roundly viewed as a shameful life choice and is portrayed as such on people's television and computer screens, even to people who don't go around searching for subversive views. Matalulu, though it breaks her heart, files for divorce and sings about it in the cabaret. Bahena distances herself from him. Saho isn't sure what's going on, but he senses a bad psychic smell emanating from his father for reasons he can't begin to fathom and steers vaguely clear. In the depths of ignominy, Bapa Jim turns himself yellow with drink and hangs himself, dies in a drowning accident, is found in an alley, crashes a private plane, shoots himself twice in the head, a rare but plausible event since a first shot can easily go amiss and cause injury but leave a man alive and capable of trying again. History remembers him in infamy.

Or no. Bapa Jim stops telling lies. He has an epiphany. After continuing on his course and stirring up trouble, he pauses one night, swirls his short glass of single malt, admires the caramel color of it, gazes at the city through the glass of the sixtieth-floor bar of a swank hotel, ponders the effects of the causes he has set in motion, smiling at first, pleased with himself, a plan conceived well and executed to perfection, takes a sip, sets his glass down, feels the impulse to ignore the feeling that quietly darkens his sensitivities, but then decides to allow it, to look it squarely in the eye like a man, to tease it out and examine it, and as he does so the smile fades from his face, the well-executed plan a horror, a nightmare, an ugliness, he reels from it, actually gasps, sits back, eyes wide, his shaking hand covering his mouth, he whispers the word *no*, lets out an anguished howl and stands up, fingers clawing at his own scalp as if to tear his hair out from the roots, staggering around the bar, attracting attention, knocking a wine glass off a woman's table with his elbow, causing her to lean back on her stool in alarm, causing the bartender to hasten to his side and find the line between helping and threatening, Jim begins to laugh the madman's laugh but there at the brink he finds the beginnings of serenity, he collects himself, he straightens his hair and his clothes, he apologizes to the bartender, he smiles again, a more bashful smile, he apologizes to the woman, gives reassuring looks to the gawkers, pays his bill, including a new glass of wine for the lady, leaves, goes home, calls his children, makes love to his wife, makes international phone calls, undoes what has been done, facilitates mutually beneficial non-exploitative trade agreements, urges everyone to remain in the warm embrace of the kind and the gentle, puts the world's genius to work toward ameliorating suffering and providing for the many, and tells the following joke:

I call my father, bless him, ninety-four years old, still driving and I warn him, I said Dad, it's on the news, seriously be careful, there's a crazy driver out there right now near your house on the interstate going the wrong way. My dad laughs at me like I'm naive. Son, he says, it's way worse than that. I'm on the interstate right now and I can tell you it's not just one guy – *everybody* is going the wrong way!

# Chapter Forty-Three

So, Saho has gone into a "tunnel" of some sort. Metaphorical? Not so fast. There is in fact nothing more common than tunnels, and not only in urban areas. Without networks of tunnels beneath our streets there would be no high-speed fiber-optic cables to the home, to say nothing of gas, electric, and water supplies and sewage disposal. The tunnels housing these utilities may be invisible, but they are entirely ubiquitous in suburban as well as urban environments and they are only the most obvious tip of the tunnel iceberg. With only the slightest effort of imagination and a cognizance of the millions of sinkholes around the world, especially in areas underlain by carboniferous limestone, at least one of which threatened to swallow a police station, which is a federal crime, it is really incumbent upon the mature philosopher of life to realize and accept that we now live in an age where the miracle is less falling into a hole and landing in a system of tunnels than going through one's entire life without it happening at least once.

Once one becomes tunnel-aware there is no turning back. Most major cities have vast networks of secret and abandoned subterranean tunnels that go far beyond the simple provision of ordinary services. London has so many acknowledged and unacknowledged tunnels that it's a wonder any of the above-ground city still has enough solid earth beneath it to support its weight. There's the Postmaster General's clandestine tunnel beneath the Old War Office, complete with bunkers, air-raid shelters, gears, and lifts connecting to a network with octopus-like arms that emerge into a variety of government buildings and telephone exchanges, extending at least six kilometers to a place where one can emerge out of an access shaft onto a traffic island in the middle of a public highway. Researchers have found bricked-off passages through which sounds and lights have filtered, suggesting that the network has and still secretly uses even more levels, deeper levels than have been publicly acknowledged.

Subterranean passages, ducts, tubes, chambers, catacombs, escape paths: these are common features not just of London, of course, but of many, perhaps most, cities. Nottingham, Edinburgh, Newcastle upon Tyne, Paris, Vladivostok, Beijing, Krakow, Moscow, Toronto, Portland, Montreal, Pilsen. New York extends downward almost as much as it does upward. It has entire abandoned subway stations, a deep and massive crypt for archbishops and the wealthy deceased, numerous abandoned train lines including a sidelined freight train tunnel turned into a graffiti masterpiece, and an underground escape tunnel in Chinatown for gangsters and gamblers in need of swift and secure exit strategies. A city without a secret underground life echoing with history along miles of caverns and tunnels is hardly a city at all.

Still, we have only scratched the surface of below-the-surface. We have not yet discussed entire underground cities, to say nothing of entire networks of interconnected underground cities. We have not yet discussed Derinkuyu in Nevsehir Province, Turkey. We have not yet discussed Kaymakli in Central Anatolia.

Perhaps Saho has stumbled into an access point to Derinkuyu, the former Elengubu. Who knows how long its tendrils reach? Who knows how many layers? It is at least eighty-five meters deep and its known contours are large enough to house twenty thousand people with room for their livestock as well, and for food stores. It has at least eighteen levels, each of which can be closed off separately by monolithic rolling stone doors, the whole of its ancient Byzantine structure closed off to the world from the inside. Huge store rooms, stables, cellars with wine and oil presses, vast dining rooms, schools, bath houses, and chapels lie beneath its barrel-vaulted ceilings. Nearly three thousand years old, it was eventually abandoned and only rediscovered when a local man found a mysterious space behind a wall while renovating his home. Let us call him Ahmet. Ahmet had chickens. The chickens would disappear. Where did they go? Why did they go? Ahmet did not know. One day finally he saw one furtively slip into a small crevasse in the wall of a lower room, looking both ways. It was by trying to retrieve his wandering flock that Ahmet discovered the first dark passageway into the labyrinth.

Eventually more than six hundred other private homes housing six hundred other Ahmets were found to have hidden entrances to the secret dominion ensconced within the earth. God only knows how many fowl had entered this alternate universe first, perhaps to make their way on their own, perhaps finding each other by clucking and waddling, perhaps huddled together in the darkness, perhaps learning to speak and make tools and build fires.

Nor was Derinkuyu unique, nor did it exist in underground isolation. It was connected by five miles of additional tunnels to Kaymakli, the former Enegup, itself consisting of hundreds of tunnels and self-contained entirely underground. Nor is that the end of it. We have not yet discussed Özkonak or Mazıköy or any of the other two hundred – yes, two hundred – underground cities sprawling for hundreds of miles and connected to each other by elaborate systems of tunnels.

These places are real. This is the world in which we live. If Ahmet can do it, so can Saho.

# Chapter Forty-Four

It was good when Aunt Gina would come in sometimes late at night. It's not that Matalulu never had fun when she was a mere slip of a little girl. She went to school; she had friends; they played; there was exuberance. But then she had to go home again.

Matalulu's mother was gentle and good, but she died young. Once in perhaps a melodramatic mood she blamed her husband's meanness for her rapidly failing health. Why had she married such a man? It's what people did in those days. He must've squeezed out an ounce of charm at some point, and the source must have dried up after that. She'd made the best of it. She'd loved her children. She had imparted values. Eventually, however, the children were left alone with their father.

Matalulu's father would punish them for the slightest of what he considered offenses, such as failure to say excuse me after a small burp, or not calling him sir when addressing him, or leaving something untidy, or getting their clothes dirty. His punishments were strange. He would make them jump from the third step onto the concrete basement floor in bare feet, again and again.

If his estranged sister, Gina, a mitigating force, did not exist, Matalulu probably would have had to invent her.

Sometimes, in the post-bedtime quiet of her own room, her feet still stinging because she hadn't eaten all of her dinner, Matalulu would receive a visit from Aunt Gina. Gina was normally just coming back from somewhere or just about to leave, which meant she always had a story. She always wore a hat. She'd come in trailing scarves, carrying bags, and she'd tell of spectacular sights, charismatic characters, dubious suitors, cowardly traitors, would-be assassins. She told of her experiences as a *diseuse*, which looks like a misspelling of disease but is actually the word for a female monologist. Aunt Gina practiced the art of the *diseuse* right there in Matalulu's room. She was a consummate storyteller. She'd also leave Matalulu exotic artifacts, fascinating curios from Timbuktu, Kashmir, Derinkuyu.

"If you were a decent person," said Matalulu, "you'd take me with you on one of these trips."

"I never said I was a decent person."

"Hm."

"Where would you want to go?"

This is where, in young Matalulu's imagination, Aunt Gina would wink and take her to the window and tell her to look outside. She would look, and just outside the window would be a hot air balloon with a dapper little gentleman pilot in the basket holding out his hand to help her get inside. Then a song would break out and Matalulu would sing it.

Or Aunt Gina would tell her she could fly if only she'd believe, and it would take some doing but eventually she'd let herself fall out of the window and the wind would pick her up and she'd sail over the treetops and say *I'm doing it, I'm doing it, I'm really doing it.* Then a song. Music would swell out of nowhere and Matalulu would deliver.

That sort of thing. Stupid stuff.

But instead, the door would fly open and her father would be angry, telling Aunt Gina it was too late for visitors. In which case Aunt Gina would stand and speak in a perfectly calm and firm tone of voice, without quavering. She'd point a strong index finger at Matalulu's father, poking him twice in the chest with it; it wouldn't even bend. Matalulu's father would react badly. He'd raise his hand, but Aunt Gina wouldn't cower. She'd stare right at him, put her hands on her hips, dare him to strike her. He would hesitate, already defeated. He'd clench his fist impotently only to drop it to his side. He'd turn and leave unsatisfied, muttering some unconvincing words. Aunt Gina would smile and shake her head. Total victory. There would never have been any doubt. Fearlessness. She'd turn to Matalulu and give her a wink. Matalulu would hold it tightly.

# Chapter Forty-Five

The unexpected discovery that Aunt Gina may have had professional experience as a *diseuse* instigated a flurry of new research, the first results of which are beginning to emerge in the literature. It seems that Yvette Xandora – a *nom de scène* – made quite a name for herself in Paris cabarets with her Belle Epoque-inspired "patter songs": pieces that were spoken or intoned rather than sung. In a series of letters to the performer, who was indeed billed as a *diseuse* on surviving posters from the day, an infatuated minor English painter wrote to her as "my dearest Gina" with confessions of love that suggested a certain mutual intimacy. Research attention has focused on this Yvette-Gina in the absence of other Gina-*diseuses* in the relevant period. Findings have been tantalizing to say the least.

Yvette-Gina was born into a poor family living in the eighteenth arrondissement neighborhood of Barbès. A happy child with sad eyes, she sang frequently, if quietly, to an imagined far-off audience somewhere in the cumulonimbus region of Europe. At the age of sixteen she took up a job as a model in the Printemps department store, where she was discovered by a self-identified journalist who, evidently, had a keen interest in sixteen-year-old girls. Whatever suspicions this scenario may conjure in the modern mind, there is no evidence to suggest that any untoward activities ensued. We do know that as a result of this introduction, Yvette-Gina took acting and diction lessons and was soon appearing on stage at small venues and by her early twenties she was headlining shows in Montmartre at the Moulin Rouge.

From contemporary accounts we know that she usually dressed all in bright yellow with long black opera gloves and that she stood almost perfectly still while performing, except for her arms, which waved like tentacles as if to express in cephalopodic sign language what mere words could not. She was described as very youthful in appearance, indeed "of virginal aspect." She was pale and slender and eschewed the rouge favored by most of her fellow performers. Audience interest seemed to have been piqued by the contrast between her innocent appearance and the ribaldry of her lyrics, full of double entendres that were described in newspapers as nothing short of "horrific." Her raunchy takes on lost love are credited with rewriting the rules of music-hall performance, and she gained notoriety not only in Paris but as far away as Brussels, London, and New York.

Famous psychiatrists from the world over came to see her perform. Hostesses vied to have her attend their parties, and she once gave a performance at a private event on the Riviera for a young prince who would later be the king called Bertie. He reportedly stood with his trouser legs pressed in an innovative side-to-side fashion and clapped his young hands together rapidly.

There's no tragic ending here. She went on to publish two novellas about the demimonde, now sadly out of print, and an instructional manual about how to speak a song. In her declining years she ran a school for girls.

That is approximately all we know for certain. How likely is it that this is the Aunt Gina we've been after all along? Although there is as usual precious little in the way of hard evidence to tie her genetically to our own Matalulu, from a statistical perspective we may legitimately speak of probabilities.

For example, it is possible to dump a bowl of five hundred pennies on the floor and have them all come up heads. However, the probability of that happening is obviously vanishingly small, although calculable (it is one in a billion billion billion billion billion billion billion or so). Whether one believes this is our Aunt Gina may well be a function of how comfortable one is around statisticians.

# Chapter Forty-Six

"So, Mister...."

"Saho," replied a startled Saho, snapping back to the present moment and remembering his sense of decorum.

"Saho, yes. Thank you for coming in to meet with us today."

"Not at all. It's a pleasure to have this opportunity."

"Would you like a glass of water? Cup of coffee? Tea?"

"No, thanks, I'm fine, really."

"Something stronger?"

"I beg your pardon?"

"A whiskey? Shot of vodka? A pill or injection of some kind?"

Trick question. Saho narrowed his eyes.

"No, thank you. I'm fine. Really. Thank you."

The interviewer jotted down some notes.

"Mr. Saho, I'm going to ask you some questions and I'd like you just to say the first answer that comes into your head."

"All right."

"Blue."

"Not a question."

"Correct. Or is it?"

"There could be some sense in which the word blue was a question."

"Such as?"

"Well, it begs the question, why blue? Blue itself poses a question by its existence. Blue questions everything that is blue and everything that is not blue. Indeed, questions themselves, if I may say, come out of the blue."

"Wrong."

"Or is it?"

"Mr. Saho, why do you want to become a mole man?"

Saho had prepared for this one. All interviews are the same. They'll ask you why you want to work there and you have to say anything but that you need a gig. They'll ask you about challenges you've overcome and what your weaknesses are and you have to give them a weakness that's actually a strength, like you're prone to working too hard, but then you let them know you've found a healthy way of dealing with it, such as by making and respecting work-life boundaries. Then you've sucked up to them but instantly also told them to back the hell off of your boundaries in a way that they're virtually forced to approve of.

"Well as you may know, I spent some time in the tunnels. Quite a lot of time, and I can tell you my eyes got so used to the dark that I couldn't even think about light after a while. Which in some ways was a challenge and a weakness that I had to overcome through a kind of moral resolve, which I lacked. And then I met some mole men and they were friendly although at the time I didn't understand any of it and I still don't understand it."

"And why do you want to become a mole man?"

Alert! Alert! Alert! In interviews, if the interviewer repeats a question, it means you haven't actually answered it to his or her satisfaction the first time around. It is a danger sign, a sign that it is time to focus, time to give the answer they want, no hemming and hawing, no dissimulating, no vagaries, just a targeted killer answer that knocks the question out of the old ballpark. Wake up. Destroy this question.

"I do not want to become a mole man."

"Go on. Say it."

"I already am a mole man."

More jotting, with nodding this time.

"And now I have a question for you!" said Saho.

The interviewer raised his fantastic eyebrows and wrinkled his deathly pale white forehead.

"OK. Let's hear it."

"What would be a good question to ask you right now?"

"Would you like a glass of water now."

"Would you like a glass of water now?"

"No, thank you."

"No, thank you too."

"Where do you see yourself in six years if not dead or in prison?"

A nice twist on the old chestnut. *Six* years indeed.

"In the tunnels, certainly."

"How deep into the tunnels?"

"Deep. I would say thirty thousand feet, plus. I would say the point at which the center of the earth becomes hollow."

"Mm hm."

Nodding, jotting.

"Talk me through your skill set and how you see it applying as a mole man."

"I get lost."

"Go on."

"I just keep going, and as I say I've gone deep. I'm not one to panic. I am comfortable lost in the dark. It's a space that I, well I'd say I've made that lonely place my own. Does that make me anti-social? I'm going to say no."

"Certainly. Now I'd like to talk about your sexual history."

"Well, OK."

"This is fine. We are mole men."

"Good."

"And has there ever been anyone special? A relationship of any significance?"

"This is important for the job?"

"This is mole man stuff."

"Do you know what's funny?"

"Tell me."

"My pecker has shrunk," whispered Saho.

"Is that what you call it? A pecker?"

"I don't think I usually call it that."

"And how does it make you feel?"

"Baffled more than anything, I suppose."

"And why on earth are you making this inappropriate and appalling confession in the middle of a job interview? What on earth made you think that was a good idea?"

"Oh, Jesus!"

"You just thought, oh, I know what's a good thing to bring up with this person interviewing me for a job – my pecker."

"No! My God, I don't know what I was thinking. I thought we were intimately sharing!"

"It's fine."

"Is it?"

"Yeah, it's mole man stuff to be honest. Also, to lie."

"Jesus. OK. You got me."

Pencil scratchings.

"Right," said the interviewer, standing up. He was tall for a mole man, a good four foot one, and thin, unbelievably thin. He laced his bony fingers together and stretched them out, cracking his bony knuckles, and then stretched over to his left side, then to his right, before circling his hips and letting out a great big yawn.

# Chapter Forty-Seven

Bahena had reached a patience-testing level of comfort with her clients. Based on their earlier feedback, she had succeeded in complaining less, but she still regularly provided the clients with plentiful background information on her life and state of mind. They listened as it went on and on. She had been a theater major at university. Her grades in high school had consistently hovered near the upper part of the range below honor roll. Her behavior, always exemplary. They listened. They listened to stories they'd rather not have heard about Bahena's first intimate experience with a boy. After university she made a brief attempt at becoming an actor. It had been fun. It fizzled out eventually. Bahena was a little bit older now all of a sudden and she realized that her side job, her day job, her pay-the-bills gig was kind of her main thing now. She was that person. It wasn't a disguise.

The clients intervened with a noise like a dolphin trying to blow up a balloon, which Bahena understood. We appreciate, it meant, that you are old enough to wonder about being old and alone. Old and alone and frightened, having wasted everything, having nothing but squandered possibility. Even the special skills we have taught you have not made you feel special, have felt only like a gift you did nothing to deserve, even though they were given from a place of love and affection. You have arrived at the point where the rising curve flattens out and starts to head downward and the might-bes are all becoming might-have-beens. It makes you feel foolish and ashamed like you were dreaming you were at a party and then the lights came on and it was an empty room, and it was cold, and even if anyone were really there, nobody would have even cared enough to mock you, and it is the utterness of that irreproachable silence that...

"All right already," said Bahena, which the clients understood as meaning they had been thanked for their useful and insightful commentary.

Bahena went home to her haunted house and sat in the downstairs room, the one that had the door to the basement. She thought she heard singing. Not just any singing. She thought she heard Johnny Mathis and he was singing When Sunny Gets Blue. There was also the sound of wind and a kind of ghostly knocking that went through all the walls in the house. The small television wasn't on, and neither was the big one upstairs. No, the Mathis sounded like it was coming from the basement.

She took a step toward the basement door but just as she started to get the feeling that it was a bad idea the basement door flew open and a silent jackie quickly enveloped her and dragged her down the stairs and into the darkest rear recesses where the boiler was.

# Chapter Forty-Eight

When the children were small, Bapa Jim would sometimes try to teach them a few things about the newspaper advertising game, at which he was by then already an old hand. He had his regular clients: the A&P, Klein's, Hill's. What he would do, as he explained to young Bahena and Saho, would be to go round to each place in person on a weekly basis, smile, shake some hands, engage in some chitchat, remember to call the checkout girl by name and tell her she was doing a bang-up job, and never be the first one to suggest that they get down to business. He'd leave that to the manager, and then he'd cheerfully agree, excusing himself while calling the deli counter man by name. Clockwork. Poetry in motion. Like it could continue this way forever.

"What are you doing now, Bapa?"

"Layout!" said Bapa Jim. "Look."

Jim had spread out a tabloid-sized piece of translucent paper and was arranging little cut-outs all over it. This was going to be an ad for the butcher's department at Hill's. A picture of lamb chops, top left. Top round on the right. Ribs, ready for the barbecue, right in the middle of the page. Chicken thighs, bottom left. Finally, the eye settles lower right, final straw on the back of anyone still on the fence, juicy thick-cut sirloin steaks. Next to each picture, a this-week-only super-low price-per-pound announced with exclamation points in the center of a multi-pointed excitement star. Overseeing the whole panoply, Bob Janovas, the butcher himself, arms outstretched at the top of the page, a can-you-even-believe-it smile beaming out of his own likably goofy face.

"The art of sales," said Bapa Jim, waving his hand over the layout. "In both senses."

"It's really nice, Bapa," said Bahena.

"It is," agreed Saho. "I mean, it's not Picasso."

"Picasso! Tell you something about Picasso. They thought he was stillborn. Yep. He was tiny and silent. He comes out, they look at him and think no, that's no good. A real shame. They put him aside. Lay him right on a side table and tend to the mother. His uncle the doctor was in the room. He's smoking a cigar. In the delivery room. This is in Spain."

"That doesn't sound very good for the babies."

"Doesn't sound good? It saved Picasso's life! The kid started coughing. It brought him around!"

Then as he glued the layout into place, he'd tell them stories: the time when Napoleon Bonaparte was once attacked by rabbits during a hunt; the one about how ketchup was originally sold as a medicine; and the one about the shortest war in history, a thirty-eight-minute affair between Britain and Zanzibar in 1896 over reluctance to submit to imperial authority.

But that was all a million years ago. Bapa Jim smiled and tuned in to the present moment. What if, he thought, a disturbance was organized in the Combined Principalities? In one of the major cities, for example. Perhaps Schmäden-Croyden, an important city on an important river, a renowned spa town, a model of clean energy industries, and crucially, a border city. What if some hoodlums, who were used to causing trouble, could be induced to cause enough trouble to warrant an intervention by the Kaiser? If he sends in the police or, better still, a national guard force or army reserves, the stories would write themselves. Authoritarianism run amok. Forces at the border. Humanitarian crisis.

Hoodlums. Brawls, property damage, mayhem. The winds howling. Naturally it might not go according to Bapa Jim's expectations at all.

"If we go in there with truncheons and tear gas," the Kaiser would likely say, "it would only make things worse."

"It is already violent," his advisor would impatiently urge. "One can't wish it away."

The Kaiser would chuckle and pat his advisor, whom he considered a friend, on the back with seasoned gentleness.

"Indeed. And we shall send in the smallest possible force of ninjas skilled in the art of quickly immobilizing multiple opponents without harming them in the least and doing it all so stealthily you'd hardly know it was even happening. You'd just think things were starting to calm down. Secondly, we will send in teams of excellent listeners and more cakes and sweets and cups of tea than you have ever seen in your life. Do you hear me?"

"And if it doesn't matter? If there's a full-scale military invasion on this pretext?"

"In that case we'll inform the citizenry and get ready to implement the Unified Civil Disobedience protocols. They want to invade, fine. Let's see how they like our stubbornly resolute forms of nonviolent resistance. I expect they'll find us a very irritating place to occupy once we've clogged the roads with carnivalesque revelries and engaged in acts of sabotage, sit-down strikes, and scathing satire. Soon enough, changing their minds and going home again will be their better option."

"This is leaderly, if I may presume to say, sir."

The Kaiser would smile, and in that simple act affirm his existence.

All of this would be picked up by human and signals intelligence and delivered to Bapa Jim on another continent. He would enter a chamber of the elite waving his dossier, making sure to make jokes and set everyone at ease and be amiable and ensure they'd all be inclined to agree with whatever it was he was going to tell them. He would look at his dossier and its account of the Kaiser's small force of peaceful listeners assembling near the border, and he would describe it as a mobilization. Everyone knows what mobilization means. Mobilization means war. What does mobilization mean? War. Everyone knows it.

"Gentlemen," he'd begin. "The Combined Principalities have mobilized forces at the border."

On everyone's insides the tolling of a somber bell would sound and the laws themselves would tremble.

# Chapter Forty-Nine

"Johnny, no!" yelled Matalulu, holding onto her hat, her hair and her scarf blowing backwards as the two-tone Ford Fairlane Sunliner convertible went screeching around the corner with the smell of burning rubber in the air. "Johnny, slow down!"

"No time for that now, baby," said the singularly resonant tenor, the legendary Johnny Mathis, as the latest bullets from the police flew past close enough to their heads for them to hear the hot whistle.

"Why'd you do it, Johnny?"

"Had to, baby."

"But why, Johnny, why?"

"A man doesn't do things," he said, taking the next reckless careening turn at high speed, "then things don't get done."

"Let me out! Let me out of this car!"

Mathis smiled the tight little smile of a man who's gone too far as he gunned the engine and took the Sunliner through a narrow alley, knocking over bins and boxes and causing people to leap out of his way at the last moment.

"I'd love to, baby," he said, still smiling tight, swerving onto a busy high street and plowing through a fruit-and-balloon stand sending colors flying everywhere, "I just can't quite do that for you right now."

"You've got to turn yourself in, Johnny!" pleaded Matalulu. "Just turn yourself in before somebody gets killed!"

"Everybody wants to be a gangster," laughed the master of impeccable silky phrasing, "until it's time to do gangster stuff."

It wasn't a kidnapping. She'd gone with him voluntarily, that much was true. Everyone can make up their own minds about whether that little move was forgivable or not. But what seemed at first like an exhilarating impromptu adventure in the company of the sultry singer whose style defies easy categorization had gotten, to put it mildly, out of control. When they went into the bank, she thought he was just making a quick deposit. Nobody was more surprised than Matalulu when he reached into his charcoal cashmere jacket and pulled out a snub-nosed .38 Special, but by the time they left the place they were running and she was, whether she liked it or not, an accomplice to an armed robbery.

Now all she wanted was just to go home. Was it still possible?

They were heading straight for the pier. A couple of steel runners used for loading trucks had been left one end up on a short stack of crates, and Johnny Mathis was heading straight for them. He wasn't slowing down. He was going to take the Sunliner airborne in hopes of landing it on a nearby barge. It wasn't going to happen. The boat was too far away. He wasn't going to have enough speed. Mathis floored it, threw his head back, and laughed like a madman.

# Chapter Fifty

In a midtown high-rise that had long been rumored to house more than just ordinary boring offices, Bahena's clients were stirring. They were making sounds like blue whales on cornets, working their tiny fingers on invisible devices, and emanating ripple waves that made structures a hundred miles away wobble as if in a large-magnitude earthquake, while leaving those nearby seemingly unaffected.

Bapa Jim experienced these waves as an uncharacteristic tightening of his chest that resulted in a slight difficulty in breathing and a nagging sense of a darkness patiently chewing at the center of his existence waiting for all the noise to die down, waiting no matter how long it took, waiting until waiting itself was the only thing left.

The French army experienced it as consensual dreamwork, in which time slowed down and objects became heavy, too heavy to move, too heavy to carry, and plans became memories through a haze of dementia and were soon forgotten in favor of the fascinations of the present moment while plopping down wherever one happened to be. People's grins threatened to pull all the skin back from their skulls.

The English army experienced high winds and saw many old trees crack and bring down telephone lines tethered to houses, causing the houses to come loose from their moorings and rise on tornado streams and settle back down but not in their former places, so that the people at number five now lived where number three once was, and everyone got used to it.

The Russians and Americans began to melt into each other and the shapes became rounder and wetter and pooled finally until they sank into the soil and came out on the other side of the world where it was cool and the moonlight made them beautiful.

Europe's rivers experienced the transmutation as if sound itself were turning on and off intermittently and getting out of sync with light, so that adjacent wetlands communicated via sub-rosa root tapping. Future historians would attribute the swamp-sinking of entire Polish battalions to this phenomenon.

Everywhere at once it became four o'clock in the afternoon and nobody knew what to eat, too early for dinner, too late for lunch. The clients kept turning knobs and pushing buttons and concentrating. Bapa Jim was consumed by mournful visions, hunched shapes loading prone shapes onto gangplanks. Then there was a great high-pitched sound in everyone's ears all over the world, which turned into radio static, and then snatches of songs, and then a silence so complete that even people with tinnitus lost their high-pitched background noise and heard absolutely nothing at all. People were mesmerized by the nothingness. So serene.

# Chapter Fifty-One

Bapa Jim, seeming distant if not shell-shocked, was cooking. It was dinner time again and the whole family was there. He had made one of his specialties: leftover spaghetti with a fried egg on top. He learned it from his father before him and he had taught it to his own children. The first time he had tried to make it, he'd made the rookie mistake of using new, first-day spaghetti. He proudly told his dad.

"I made your specialty: fried egg on spaghetti!"

"Leftover spaghetti?" his father had said, looking up from his newspaper with a frown because he was quite sure there hadn't been any.

"No," Bapa Jim had admitted. "It was new spaghetti."

His father shook his head.

The first time Saho made it, he made the same rookie mistake and received the same correction, causing Bapa Jim once again to appreciate the rhyme scheme of history. Bahena got it right the first time.

Bapa Jim wore a flat smile and put spaghetti on plates. It was spaghetti from two days earlier. The sauce was all mixed in, soaked up, saturated. Minimalist. It wasn't swimming in sauce.

"Wait, wait, wait," he said, warning people off any notions they might have had of digging in before the fried egg had been applied.

People were free to add grated parmesan now or they could wait. Bapa Jim approached with the frying pan, eggs still sizzling in hot brown butter.

"These are just perfect," he said, gently working his spatula underneath one of the four trembling eggs. "Over easy but not too runny, not too thick. They're in the Goldilocks zone."

He dropped the first egg on Matalulu's plate.

"Look at that," he said. "That's beautiful. That's perfect."

He said the same thing when he dropped the second egg on Bahena's spaghetti, and he said it again when he dropped the third on Saho's plate. The fourth egg had a busted yolk and he saved it for his own plate. He thought first of others. It made no difference to him. And he was determined not to recognize that each of them was some sort of phantom version of themselves. Variously waxen, ghostly, translucent, enshrouded. Take your pick.

"Pop's Spaghetti," he announced proudly before returning the frying pan to the cooker and sitting down at the table. "A finer meal you'll never find. Dig in. One time when I was young, I added sausages to the mix. Thinking of it now, I wish we had some. Hey. You know my friend Ned? The guy who married the blind lady? No? Well, he did, and she just told him she's seeing someone. He's trying to figure out if that's great news or awful."

Bahena laughed. Her nose quivered.

"I don't really know a guy named Ned," said Bapa Jim. "I wish I did."

*I'm talking too much*, thought Bapa Jim, *and not enough*.

The edges of Matalulu's mouth lifted in curls suggestive of a smile. Saho hadn't moved. A fly landed on his nose. Flew off again. His waxen head seemed to be held on with picture nails.

There was reflection then, for a moment, and chewing. Nothing like a little bit of quiet chewing time at dinner.

Ding dong, came the knock at the door. Who could it be? A delivery? Did you or you or you order anything? No, neither did I! A salesman? A religious scholar? A petitioner? A fundraiser? A visitor? Bahena's head moved unless it was just a trick of the light. Whatever it was, it made her father decide to go to the front door as if it were a race, just because it was playful and funny to do so, as if they'd have to jostle each other on the way to try to be the first one to get to the door. Matalulu's head seemed to turn slightly at an inquisitive angle but it may have just been shadows or an outbreak of static noise. Saho's face was slack and placid and one of the picture nails fell out of his neck. Bapa Jim won his race against nobody and got to the door first and opened it wide, smiling to the point of laughing, recovering with feigned embarrassment in front of the tall pale woman at the door holding out her white-gloved hand.

"Aunt Gina," said the woman, eyes bright and piercing, hands firmly on hips. After a stunned silence she added: "Aren't you going to invite me in?"

Matalulu's mouth edges smiled higher and a tear rolled out of her eye. A real tear.

# Author Biography

John Schoneboom is the award-winning author of the novel *Fontoon* (Dedalus Books), the nonfiction work *Surrealpolitik* (Zer0 Books), and a number of plays produced for Off Off Broadway venues. He is the founding editor of Bratum Books' *Uncommonalities* series of short stories that share a common first line, supported in part by a grant from the Catherine Cookson Charitable Trust. Originally from New York, Schoneboom now resides in Newcastle upon Tyne.

## Also by John Schoneboom

### Novels
*Fontoon*
(Dedalus Books, 9781909232891)

### Nonfiction
*Surrealpolitik: Surreality and the National Security State*
(Zer0 Books, 9781785359491)

### Short Stories
*Uncommonalities Volume I: A Taste for It*
(Bratum Books, 9781838173715)
*Uncommonalities Volume II: Bad Enough*
(Bratum Books, 9781838173708)
*Uncommonalities Volume III: Accident*
(Bratum Books, 9781838173722)
*Uncommonalities Volume IV: Eventually*
(Bratum Books, 9781838173753)
*Uncommonalities Volume V: Nobody*
(Bratum Books, 9781838173760)

ROUNDFIRE
BOOKS

# FICTION

Put simply, we publish great stories. Whether it's literary or popular, a gentle tale or a pulsating thriller, the connecting theme in all Roundfire fiction titles is that once you pick them up you won't want to put them down.
If you have enjoyed this book, why not tell other readers by posting a review on your preferred book site.

## The Cause
Roderick Vincent
The second American Revolution will be a
fire lit from an internal spark.
Paperback: 978-1-78279-763-0 ebook: 978-1-78279-762-3

## Don't Drink and Fly
The Story of Bernice O'Hanlon: Part One
Cathie Devitt
Bernice is a witch living in Glasgow. She loses her way
in her life and wanders off the beaten track looking for the
garden of enlightenment.
Paperback: 978-1-78279-016-7 ebook: 978-1-78279-015-0

## Gag
Melissa Unger
One rainy afternoon in a Brooklyn diner, Peter Howland
punctures an egg with his fork. Repulsed, Peter pushes
the plate away and never eats again.
Paperback: 978-1-78279-564-3 ebook: 978-1-78279-563-6

## The Master Yeshua
The Undiscovered Gospel of Joseph
Joyce Luck
Jesus is not who you think he is. The year is 75 CE. Joseph
ben Jude is frail and ailing, but he has a prophecy to fulfil ...
Paperback: 978-1-78279-974-0 ebook: 978-1-78279-975-7

### On the Far Side, There's a Boy
Paula Coston
Martine Haslett, a thirty-something 1980s woman, plays hard on the fringes of the London drag club scene until one night which prompts her to sign up to a charity. She writes to a young Sri Lankan boy, with consequences far and long.
Paperback: 978-1-78279-574-2 ebook: 978-1-78279-573-5

### Tuareg
Alberto Vazquez-Figueroa
With over 5 million copies sold worldwide, *Tuareg* is a classic adventure story from best-selling author Alberto Vazquez-Figueroa, about honour, revenge and a clash of cultures.
Paperback: 978-1-84694-192-4


Readers of ebooks can buy or view any of these bestsellers by clicking on the live link in the title. Most titles are published in paperback and as an ebook. Paperbacks are available in traditional bookshops. Both print and ebook formats are available online.

Find more titles and sign up to our readers' newsletter, visit:
www.collectiveinkbooks.com/fiction

Printed and bound by CPI Group (UK) Ltd, Croydon, CR0 4YY

20/01/2025

01823143-0005